SINCERELY, SAD DAD

Jennifer L. Davidson

ISBN: 1478313900
ISBN-13: 978-1478313908

For my parents

ACKNOWLEDGMENTS

This book would not have been possible without the support and encouragement of my husband, Kris Davidson. For allowing me to have quiet, peaceful mornings between the hours of five and seven, I'd like to thank my three children, Jax, Ilsa, and Koy. Words cannot express my gratitude to the individuals who took the time to read and comment on the draft of this manuscript: the Aune women, Nick Compiseno, Stacey Kaufman, Marsha Peterson, and Ali Wenhart. For the beautiful photograph adorning the front cover, I have Paul Pluskwik to thank.

1

To: kodyburkoff@inyourwords.com
From: sad_dad1@gmail.com
Subject: Stop my compulsion to kill

Dear Ms. Burkoff,

I came across your website the other night and am interested in obtaining your services. My daughter, Julia, was murdered almost a year ago. She meant the world to me as I'm sure you do to your father. I don't mean to shock you, but ever since her death I haven't been able to rid myself of the urge to stalk and kill the boy that carelessly took her life. He should be rotting in jail or lying on the side of the road for all I care. Instead, the judge ruled her death an accident, which means that this shameless boy is running around enjoying life and looking forward to the future. Even after all these months, I see red thinking about him and about how my daughter no longer has a future.

Counseling, reading books, and facing my demons head on, I've done it all. Nothing seems to rid me of the anger and grief I'm harboring inside. Then I had an idea. What if I have a memoir written about my life with my sweet girl so that when I get those dark thoughts I can remind myself of the happiness she brought to me and her mother? It can't hurt, right? Maybe this will save that boy's life and save me from becoming a prisoner for the rest of mine.

You probably think I'm a lunatic. I understand if you delete this message and try to forget my words. I know I sound desperate, even murderous. Put yourself in my shoes. What would you do? How would you feel? Where would you go for help?

I'm hoping that we can work together strictly through e-mail. Knowing what you do about me already, I doubt that you'd argue with this request. I'm not a scary man by any means. I live a normal life. I had a normal job. I have friends that I periodically socialize with. I'm simply a man having a hard time dealing with my daughter's death. That doesn't make me a bad person.

Please reply if you're willing to take a chance on a sad dad. If you do, you'll get to meet a wonderful young lady that was taken away from this world way before her time.

Sincerely,
sad dad

2

"It says what?" Kendall screamed into the phone.

Kendall has been my best friend since forever so her reaction to hearing sad dad's e-mail was no surprise.

"I'm not even joking about this. What should I do?" I asked.

"What you should do is call the police. There's a lunatic in our town and he's about to commit murder."

"He might not live in Belmont. It's called the World Wide Web for a reason, Kendall. He could be anywhere."

"Whatever. Is this the type of client you were after when you created that hack-job of a website?"

"Not exactly, but at least I know it's working."

"Well, it's not working real well if you ask me. He doesn't sound like that nice, old woman you wanted to interview."

"I know. Either way, this guy is asking for my help."

"He's asking to be arrested."

"He hasn't done anything yet. Thinking about committing a crime isn't the same as actually stabbing a knife through someone's heart. How many times have you said you wanted to beat down Jason with a stick just to knock some sense into him?"

"Every wife says that about her husband. I *would* like to beat him with a stick every once in a while."

"It's not illegal to think that way, is it? How about all those Patterson books we've read. Should James Patterson be arrested for being so damn demented in his writing?"

"I sometimes wonder." Kendall sighed. "However you want to look at it, Kody, I still think our fine men and women that work so hard to protect us might want a heads-up about a possible murderer. There is a seriously good chance this man will commit a crime."

"Okay, I see your point," I said, knowing that there wasn't much of a difference in what Kendall and I were arguing. "My initial reaction after reading the e-mail was to seize the opportunity to save two men, sad dad and the boy that he says killed his daughter. I could use my interviewing talents to turn this guy around. What if I can stop a murder from happening?"

"What if you can't, Kody? Do you want that hanging over your head for the rest of your life?"

That was definitely something to consider. How would I feel knowing that I had failed to stop a murder from happening? I'd be devastated of course. Anyone would be, especially after they were given the opportunity to try to stop it. Maybe I was crazy for thinking that by working with this man I could help him remember his daughter in all her glory, and help him get past the hateful feelings he had toward the boy who caused the fatal accident.

"But what if I can?" I asked. The image of me becoming a local hero remained at the forefront. Talk about free advertising. "What if I can help him get past the hateful feelings he has for the boy? I mean, he said it was ruled an accident. He should be able to accept that at some point."

"Kody, as a parent I can't imagine not feeling pure hatred or even having murderous thoughts toward the person that caused one of my boys' death. I'd surely want him or her to suffer the same pain, the same outcome that my son did. The question is: What would I do with those feelings? I'm pretty sure that I would never act on them, but can you say the same for sad dad? No, you can't. You don't know him from the cute guy running the gas station you frequent. There are a lot of crazies in this world and he, my friend, might just be the leader of the pack."

It took me a second to respond to Kendall. She spoke with such passion and energy when it came to her little boys. Knowing how much she loved them and how much they meant to her made me wonder if she really could share the same existence with the person that took one of them away from her.

"There certainly is a lot to think about. He might be past the point of no return. He might also be waiting for that one person to step forward to help him. What if I'm that one person?"

Kendall didn't comment.

I continued. "It's not as if I have to make a decision today. He's probably expecting me to delete the message anyway."

"I don't see how you can even consider this, Kody. To me, it's a no-brainer. You call the police and forward them the e-mail. They can deal with this nut-job. You don't want a repeat of the whole Daniel debacle, do you?"

Ugh! Why does she always have to be so practical?

"No, of course I don't want to go through that again."

Kendall was referring to Daniel, a previous client of mine, who employed my services to document the love he shared with his recently deceased wife, Maggie. Daniel loved Maggie more than anything and it was endearing to hear about the romance between them. His story matched what I was hoping to achieve for myself. I later learned that his story also had all the qualities of a spectacular *Lifetime* movie, including the part where things went completely awry and I had to be rescued. I never saw it coming; hence Kendall's opposition toward my willingness to help sad dad.

"Just be careful with this guy. I can't make the decision for you, but I'm not so sure trying to talk him out of the inevitable is in your best interest. You know I'm always looking out for you, which reminds me, Kevin stopped by my office again last Friday and asked about you. You should really consider giving him a second chance."

"You can't force chemistry, Kendall. It's either there or it isn't. Kevin and I just didn't have that. I thought we did for a while, but then we couldn't stop bickering. I felt like I was dating my brother."

"Well, I still think it might work if you gave it another chance. Let me know if you change your mind and I'll set everything up."

"You'll be the first to know." Steering the conversation away from Kevin and the rest of the men she had set me up with, I said, "Thanks for talking this sad dad thing through with me. I hope I didn't keep you from anything."

"Nah. Jason is in the garage and the boys are playing in the backyard. Our vacation week at home isn't turning out to be all that exciting. I actually have some time to myself right now and I have no idea what to do with it," Kendall said with a sigh. "Call me when you've made your decision."

Poor Kendall. Striving to be the best mom and most attentive wife was a second full-time job. I hated to hear such disappointment in her voice after she shared with me her excitement at staying home for a week to do all the things she usually missed out on. Maybe driving her two sons to their summer soccer camp wasn't as great as she thought it would be, or haggling over breakfast, lunch, and dinner was more work than she expected. Her own mother, who suffered from mental illness, was absent for a lot of her childhood so she was obviously overcompensating. Not having a female role model to compare herself to makes it all the more challenging.

Her obsession with perfection had nothing to do with why she always had to bring up Kevin's name. I heard his name more than a dozen times when I spent hours upon hours working on my hack-job of a website, as Kendall so kindly referred to it. She insisted I call him for help. I insisted I go at it on my own. Yes, I knew Kevin could and would create an amazing website with all the bells and whistles for my ghostwriting business, however, what held me back was my fear of giving him the wrong impression. I didn't want him to think that I had reconsidered our breakup. When we ended our relationship a few short months ago, it was a mutual decision. Well, mine more than his, I guess. I tried my best to make him think he wanted it as much as I did.

Putting Kevin out of my mind, I locked up the office to meet my mom for lunch. She claimed my hairstylist was worth the hundred mile trip so every six to eight weeks she took a day for herself and a little mother-daughter time. I was totally game as long as she didn't ask me about dating. That was just a fight waiting to happen.

My mom, Lynn, was already sipping an iced coffee when I arrived at the deli. Mrs. Owen, owner of the deli and distinguished town gossip, was sitting across the table from her probably spreading the latest rumor I had heard from Kendall about Hank the barber. Apparently Hank has received numerous packages in the mail from Nicaragua. Imagining the worst, someone started the rumor that he was distributing drugs to the Twin Cities. As if you could ship cocaine using the United States Postal Service.

My mom's eyes lit up when she saw me. She jumped up and gave me a big hug. My mom was a hugger.

"Hi, honey! It's so good to see you."

"It's good to see you too, Mom. When did you get here?"

"Oh, you know, about a half hour ago. I walked around the park a little since it's such a beautiful day. Then I came in here and Mrs. Owen has been keeping me company."

"Well, that's nice of you, Mrs. Owen," I said.

"I love catching up with your mom. I was also telling her to steer clear of Hank's place. Have you heard about what he's got going on?"

"Kendall filled me in the other day," I said, fighting the urge to roll my eyes. "I hate to make assumptions about those packages. I like Hank and can't imagine him doing anything illegal."

"I've always liked Hank too, but people change. I've seen it first-hand. People change for the worse and you don't see it coming. Anyway, I'll let you ladies be. Enjoy your time at the salon, Lynn."

"I certainly will," my mom replied. With Mrs. Owen out of sight, she commented to me, "That woman is too much. She shouldn't be spreading rumors like she does."

"I don't think she has anything better to do."

"That's unfortunate. She should be enjoying life, doing the things she couldn't do in her twenties and thirties, or her forties for that matter."

"Where is this coming from?"

A brilliant smile spread across my mom's face. Something was up.

I raised one eyebrow and asked, "What's going on, Mom?"

"Oh, Kody, I do have some exciting news to share with you."

I sat down across the table from her. Her news wasn't going to wait so my stomach would have to.

"Your father and I have decided to do something we have wanted to do for years, decades even. I guess I never really thought it was possible until you kids moved out. Now, though, the sky's the limit."

"Geez. I didn't know we were such a burden. You could have asked me to leave sooner."

"You'll know what I'm talking about when you have children, dear. Your father and I finally feel as if we are ready to venture off into the wild, blue yonder."

My brother, Justin, and I have been completely out of the house for almost five years now so I don't know what has taken them so long to visit that blue yonder my mom was talking about. I say completely because we each crawled back home after college when we couldn't find employment right away. Maybe my parents were hesitant to celebrate their freedom until now.

"Which wild, blue yonder are you off too?" I asked.

"We're going on an Alaskan cruise!" she said excitedly.

"Wow! That's awesome, Mom. I'm really happy for you." I reached into my purse for my wallet. "Let me grab an iced tea and a sandwich and you can tell me all about it."

As soon as I sat back down, my mom spewed out everything she knew about the cruise: the size of their room, how much extra it cost for them to have a window, what food they were apt to eat, and the activities available to them on and off the ship. From the sounds of it, she and my dad were going to have a wonderful time. I was so happy for them, yet I found myself becoming increasingly jealous. My parents, who had been married for thirty-six years, were going to spend ten glorious days together exploring a world neither they, nor I, had ever been to. What I was most envious of was that they had each other to rely on when they got lost, when they didn't have the courage to hike a few feet higher, and when one of them needed a shoulder to lean on when the water grew too rough. I longed for that companionship. I longed to have a best friend always at my side. I knew it would happen eventually. Most things happened eventually.

"Enough about me," she finally said. "How are you, Kody? You haven't called in a while. Your father thought you might have found someone special to keep you busy."

That's my mom, siphoning her curiosity through my dad.

"No one's keeping me busy except my clients."

My mom examined her manicure, which was a sure sign that she had something more to say but wasn't sure how I'd take it. I didn't beg. The woman had no will power. It would come out if I kept silent long enough. To make it even harder on her I left the table to set our cups and plates in the dirty dish bin. She looked like she might explode when I returned.

"Paul is back in town," she blurted out. "I talked to him in the market the other morning. He's divorced with no children."

That's what I had been waiting for, even if the name sent chills down my spine. Paul was someone from my past whom I hadn't thought about in an incredibly long time.

"He asked how you were doing," she added.

"What did you tell him?" I asked, feeling my eyebrows scrunch together.

"I told him about your business. He said he might look you up if he was ever in the area."

With suspicious eyes, I asked, "He did? Is that all you talked about?"

"Don't look at me like that. What else do you think we talked about? Your high school relationship didn't come up in our conversation if that's what you're wondering."

"Sorry."

"That's okay. I know you two had something special. I just wanted to prepare you in case he decided to walk into your office one of these days."

"I can't believe he's back. I figured he'd be one of those people who was too successful to return home."

"Everyone comes home sooner or later."

"I guess you're right," I said, crumpling my napkin. "Does he look the same?"

"He looks just like he did when he left, except he's filled out some. He's grown into a very handsome man."

I figured as much. Paul was adorable in high school. He was tall, a little on the skinny side, and had a face full of freckles. His strawberry blond hair grew faster than I thought was humanly possible so he always looked like he needed a trim. I liked everything about Paul, but it was his smile that won me over. He smiled with his mouth and his eyes. You know you've got a keeper then.

I've always denied being in love with Paul. I was in high school. What did I know about love? We had a lot of fun together, I knew that much. We experienced things together that I would never forget, which was why we broke up. It was also the reason for me never wanting to see him again.

"Did he mention why his marriage failed?" I asked.

"No, and I didn't ask. Marriage isn't always easy to figure out. If you don't grow and change with your partner, the marriage is likely to fail. I imagine that's what happened in Paul's case. I've seen it many times before," she said, shaking her head.

A sullen expression fell over my mom. She hated hearing about divorce. It was especially hard for her to hear about someone my age or younger getting a divorce. I, of course, thought it was because of me, although something else told me there was another reason for her strong feelings on the subject. I would never find out the real reason though. She wasn't one to share her feelings or much of anything from her past. In all honesty, I wasn't exactly sure who my mom was before she got married and had my brother and me. For all I knew, she might have got a divorce way back when. Wouldn't that be something?

Wanting to end our lunch date on a positive note, I returned the conversation to her upcoming hair appointment. Glancing at her watch, she gave me a quick run-down of what she planned to do. I already knew she'd walk out of the salon looking the same as always, but sometimes that was a good thing. We hugged good-bye on the sidewalk outside the coffee shop and she made me promise to call on the weekend to talk to my dad. He needed to hear my voice she said.

On my walk back to the office, I soaked up as much of the beautiful sunshine as I could. It was a picture-perfect day, a day that made me want to sing with the birds, dash from tree to tree with the squirrels, and float along in the breeze beside a Monarch butterfly. Nothing beat a summer day in Minnesota. On the other hand, nothing ruined a summer day more than an office door. It wasn't that I disliked my job because I loved what I did for a living. Helping people write their memoirs was my dream job. In an ideal world though, we'd all take the month of July off. There would be no need to pay the bills or go shopping. We'd all live off the land and make daily exchanges with our neighbors for provisions. It would be a month of utopia.

I was stalling. Sad dad needed an answer. What was I going to tell him?

3

I stared at the screen rereading the e-mail from sad dad. The opportunity to help a man stop himself from committing murder was exhilarating, yet horrifying. I would be willing to bet not a lot of people have been in the same situation. To help someone quit smoking, yes. To prevent someone from pulling the trigger, no. The decision weighed on me. What if I agreed to work with this man and I couldn't stop him from committing murder? Would I be in trouble for withholding information from the police? Would I feel responsible for the death of the victim? On the other hand, what if I agreed to work with sad dad and was able to help him get past the rage he was feeling? Would the fix be long-term? Would he and the boy he says killed his daughter live normal lives? What if he was hot? Sorry, that was inappropriate.

The sight of Mrs. Lopez and her puppy pal, Princess, walking across the street broke up the yo-yo conversation I was having with myself. From the looks of her she was either making a pit stop before heading off to somewhere special or she had just returned from there because she was dressed to the hilt. Not a hair was out of place, not a piece of bling was missing. It was also safe to assume that she had yet another new handbag. Almost every time she came to see me her handbag was different. I noticed this about her because part of me was jealous that I wasn't more like her in that aspect. I purchased a new handbag maybe once a year and it was a pretty big deal. It took several weeks of shopping around to choose just the right one. Knowing that I would have it for quite awhile, I didn't want to make light of this ritual.

Not only did Mrs. Lopez look good, she was feeling good too. It was evident from the proud smile she wore and the glide in her step.

"Good afternoon, Mrs. Lopez. It's so good to see you."

"Oh, hello, Kody. I hope you have a few minutes to spare for me. I have such a wonderful memory to share with you," she said, walking past me to the couches in the back of the office. Princess and I kindly followed her lead.

Mrs. Lopez, a great-grandmother, has been a client of mine for over a year because she refused to print her memoir without including a small story about everyone that was and is important to her. After about a month of her coming into my office, with or without an appointment, I realized that *every* person she met was important to her. She even had me include a story about the paper boy that ran after Princess when she took off after a squirrel. Indeed the paper boy's actions were heroic, but to include him in her memoir was a bit much. I had told her several times that she needed to stop; that some of these people she was including weren't significant enough. Honestly, I think she just liked coming into my office once or twice a week to share memories from her past. I didn't think she would ever come to me and say the memoir was finished. That was like saying she was finished, like she was giving up and was ready to say good-bye. I hoped I never had to hear that from Mrs. Lopez.

Before sitting down to "spare a few minutes," which meant at least an hour, I poured Mrs. Lopez a cup of decaffeinated coffee. Shortly after she told me about her plan for her memoir, I added an extra machine specifically for decaf. I sensed she and I were in for a long working relationship.

"You look fabulous. Another lunch date?" I asked.

"You know me. I can't sit at home for too long. A dear friend of mine invited me over for lunch so that she could tell me all about her bunion surgery. I really didn't want to hear about it, you know, but I need to support her."

"You're such a good friend."

"I try to be. This world would be a lonely place without them."

"Isn't that the truth?"

Mrs. Lopez sipped her coffee.

"So, tell me," I said, "who is this wonderful memory about that has put that brilliant smile on your face?"

"Am I still smiling?" she asked, blushing.

"It hasn't left your face yet."

"Oh, I just can't help it. I'm absolutely tickled about this one. It's about my dear Eduardo. May he rest in peace." Mrs. Lopez made a cross motion over her chest. "Saturday morning I went to the farmer's market like I do almost every Saturday in the summer. The flowers there are exquisite and I've never been much of a gardener you know."

"You've mentioned that."

"Well, as I meandered my way around the market, I came upon an older Hispanic gentleman playing beautiful music on his guitar for all the patrons. I had never seen him there before, or in town for that matter. I sauntered past him and smiled. He returned the favor. Before I got too far away, he began to play a very old song that is near and dear to my heart. I don't know the name of it, but I do remember it being the song that Eduardo and I first danced to when we started dating. Eduardo would remember the name of it. He was always good about things like that. Remembering the names of songs, cars, and movies has never been a strength of mine."

While Mrs. Lopez hemmed and hawed about the name of the song she danced to with her late husband, I took a moment to stroll down memory lane to my first school dance. What an eye opener that was. I was in the seventh grade, still extremely naïve and innocent. So innocent that when one of my friends told me about another friend letting her boyfriend go up her shirt, I asked, "Up the back?" I could not fathom why it was such a big deal that he touched her back. When I was told the boy touched her boobs, I was absolutely shocked. I could never look at that girl in the same way again.

As the night progressed, I witnessed eighth-grade couples sucking each other's air from their lungs. I remember staring at them, wondering when they were going to stop and take a breath. Occasionally, a teacher would interrupt them and pry their yearning mouths and bodies apart, only to have them stick together like Velcro when the teacher turned his back. I didn't yearn back then. I was still chasing boys around the gym and huddling with my friends while gawking at the kissers. Ah, to be that innocent again.

"…and then we kissed. It was the most magical kiss, Kody. I'll never forget it. Do you remember your first kiss?"

"Um, yeah, I think so. I remember it being wet and gross. It felt like a giant worm was squiggling around in my mouth."

"Kody!" she shouted.

I laughed at her reaction.

"Sorry, Mrs. Lopez. That's what I remember about my first kiss. It's not as if I was in love with the guy or anything. A bunch of us were playing some closet game and I got stuck with this boy who had pretty much kissed every girl in our grade. I wanted to be like everyone else so I kissed him. I didn't think it was any big deal at the time, but when I left that closet I remember feeling confused and more than a bit grossed out."

Mrs. Lopez shook her head in disgust. "It's too bad you had to experience it like that. Back in my day, you only kissed one or two boys before you got married. Look at you. You've probably kissed a hundred and you're still single."

Ouch. That hurt. From the look on Mrs. Lopez's face she knew she had crossed the line.

Simmering in my seat, I quickly calculated how many men I had actually kissed, stopping at thirty because I was also disgusted with myself. It did seem like a lot if you did a grand total, but at the time I wasn't alarmed by my behavior. Hell, I was a twenty-nine-year-old, single woman. In this day and age it would be a travesty if I hadn't kissed that many men.

"I shouldn't have said that, Kody. I'm so sorry," Mrs. Lopez said as she leaned forward to grab my hand.

I let her take it even though I didn't really want her to.

"I didn't mean to hurt your feelings. Times are different now. I hope I didn't upset you."

"I'm okay. You shocked me more than anything. And for the record, I haven't kissed a hundred men. I've kissed more than I should have and more than you would approve of, I'm sure, but not a hundred."

"Of course you haven't. No one has kissed a hundred men. Well, I'm sure some women have," she said, raising her eyebrows. When I didn't respond, she continued. "Why don't I tell you about the memory I came here to share with you?"

Also wanting to get back on track, I replied, "That sounds lovely."

"I don't know what the name of the song was, but it's a melody that I will never forget." Mrs. Lopez gazed out toward the front windows rather dreamily. "Eduardo and I continued dancing and occasionally kissing on the dance floor the rest of the night. There wasn't anything it seemed that could keep us apart. When he walked me home that night I knew he would one day be my husband. The chemistry between us was so strong."

Chemistry. There was that word again. It was the magical feeling between a man and a woman that drove them together in all ways imaginable. I've had that feeling a few times. Certainly not a hundred, mind you. In my case though, the flame quickly faded into a smoldering campfire that you couldn't even roast a marshmallow on. For some reason, I never seemed to keep that flame raging like it should. It was almost like college all over again. Everyone else was passing chemistry while I had to retake the damn class. Science just wasn't my thing. It never has been.

As Kendall said, Kevin and I had that chemistry at one time. I felt it and I liked it. I really liked it. I thought our flame would never die. With Kevin, the flame was never out of control. It was a slow burn and unusually dependable. I felt safe and secure in his flame. Then, in typical Kody fashion, the constant glow got to be too much for me. It wasn't only because we fought like my brother and I did when we were growing up, or like my dad used to say, "like two ugly school girls," it was also because the fire between Kevin and I was almost too controlled. A spark never dared to jump out of the safety circle. Didn't every woman desire a bit of danger? Was it too much to ask for that fire to occasionally get out of hand and cause some trouble? I wanted security and spontaneity. I wanted it all.

"We danced to that same song at our wedding. It was such a wonderful night. I remember it like it was yesterday. Our family and friends were gathered around us to celebrate the love we shared, the commitment we were making to each other. My grandmother sat at the head of the table swaying to beat of the music. My parents waltzed around the room catching up with friends they hadn't seen in years. My younger cousins played tag outside in the courtyard and Eduardo's brother, Antonio, flirted with my single girlfriends." She chuckled. "That man was quite the character. My youngest son, Carlos, actually reminds me of him."

"How is that?"

"The girls loved Antonio. He was exceptionally good looking and knew just what to say to them. Our wedding night was no different. I watched him dance with just about every girl in attendance, including the little ones. They giggled as he moved them around the dance floor."

"Did he find his bride that night or wasn't he the settling down type?"

"How could a man like that choose? Women of all types flocked to him. He had no intention of ever settling down. In fact, he never did get married. He had several illegitimate children, but never took a wife. He and Eduardo were so different in that way. His lack of responsibility is eventually what broke the bond of their brotherhood. Eduardo was ashamed that a man of his own blood had children running around without a father figure in their lives. Being a father was important to Eduardo. He took the job very seriously. He would have a heart attack if he knew how our Carlos behaves. He isn't much better than his Uncle Antonio."

"Some men are like that," I said. "Some women are too. Marriage isn't for everyone, but unfortunately anyone can create a child. It's too bad there isn't a way to put a restriction on an individual that has no desire to become a parent."

Mrs. Lopez nodded. She didn't like to talk about her sons' faults. In her eyes, they were perfect.

"There really aren't any more details of my story to put down on paper, Kody. The feelings I had while Eduardo held me on that dance floor are difficult to put into words. I'm surprised I even heard the song over the pounding of my heart. And then the touch of his hand while we walked home was so gentle. He had wonderful hands." She looked down at her own hands. "Mine are gnarled from old age now."

Her memory had turned her smile into a frown. Some memories had a way of doing that. She often told me stories about her late husband, Eduardo, most of which brought tears to her eyes. She truly loved that man and missed him every day that they were apart. I was under the impression that dealing with someone's death got easier over the years, but Eduardo had been gone for almost twenty years. Maybe it wasn't that it got easier, maybe it was that the tears fell less frequently. I've never lost anyone close to me yet, but I can't imagine it ever being easy to live life without them.

I handed Mrs. Lopez a tissue and reached across the coffee table to give her a hug.

"I'm fine. You know my memories of him always get to me," she said as she wiped her eyes. Princess noticed she was upset too and did her best to put a smile on her owner's face. It worked.

After a little more consoling, I walked Mrs. Lopez out to her car. I wanted to change her train of thought before she got behind the wheel. Her driving when her mind wasn't preoccupied was scary enough. We conversed briefly about the weather because that's what we did in Minnesota when we didn't know what else to talk about. The summer sun gave us only good things to say.

With Mrs. Lopez buckled up and Princess perched in the back window, I was able to concentrate on the construction truck parked in front of the vacant office space next door. It wasn't there this morning, or was it? I didn't always have an eye for the obvious. Was it possible that someone was actually moving in next to me? Unable to subdue my curiosity, I crept closer and peeked through the open door. I had been in my office space for just over a year now and this was the first time that door had been ajar. Having toured all the spaces in the building, I knew that the layout was almost identical to mine. The only reason I chose the space I did was because I distinctly remember this other one having a hint of cat odor. I knew right away that wasn't something I wanted to deal with.

"Can I help you?" asked a voice from behind me.

I jumped and gave a small yelp. What can I say? I scare easily.

Turning around, I said, "No. I was just being nosy. My office is next door." I extended my hand. "I'm Kody Burkoff, owner of *In Your Words*."

Shaking my hand, the man introduced himself. "I'm Dexter Pearl, the general contractor working on this space for the new occupant." He paused, my hand still in his. "Say, aren't you the woman I read about in the paper last winter?"

"Yes, that was me. It was a rather unfortunate event to say the least."

"He's still in jail I hope," Dexter added.

I nodded. "He'll be there for quite a few more years." Turning around to peer inside again, I said, "Regardless, it'll be nice to have a neighbor, someone within shouting distance."

Dexter smiled. "Starting tomorrow I'll have workers here for at least two weeks. The new owner has asked for a couple of upgrades, and then we need to rip out that old carpet. It smells like a herd of cats once lived in there."

"I noticed that too. Good luck with that," I said with a smirk. He didn't look like the kind of guy that liked cats too well. Honestly, I didn't know too many men that liked cats all that much. Weird.

"Well, I'll let you get back to work. I'm sure it'll look great when you're done," I said, walking away with a friendly wave good-bye.

Back inside my office, I cursed myself for not asking more questions. Why didn't I ask who or what business was going in next door? I was so bad at impromptu interrogations. I needed time to make a list of questions before having a conversation with most people. If Kendall were here, she'd have a rolodex of questions at the tip of her tongue, not leaving the man's side until her curiosity was cured. I, on the other hand, never wanted to pry into matters such as these and often left kicking myself for not being more inquisitive. What was wrong with me? Why couldn't I be more like Kendall? Unfortunately, I knew the truth. Words were just easier for me to write than speak. I hated that about myself, although being that my newest client wanted to converse strictly through e-mail, it was sometimes to my advantage.

4

To: sad_dad1@gmail.com
From: kodyburkoff@inyourwords.com
Subject: My decision

Dear sad dad,

After much deliberation, I have decided to help you place the memories of your daughter in the forefront, leaving behind those angry feelings you have for the young man you feel is responsible for her death. This decision was not an easy one as I'm sure your decision to approach me was not easy. It is with great hope that our working together will "stop your compulsion to kill." The feelings you have for your daughter and the young man that was involved are undoubtedly more intense than anything I've ever felt. I can't say that I understand how it feels to lose someone so close.

To go along with the business agreement and confidentiality contract I've attached, I thought there should be some conditions to our working relationship. I came up with the following:

1. Our communication is through e-mail only as you suggested. You may remain anonymous if you prefer.

2. If at any time you feel that our working together is doing more harm than good, please end our relationship. I will understand.

3. If your compulsion to kill becomes greater, please call the police or seek professional help. I can suggest names.

The last item left to discuss is when to start. When you're ready, introduce me to your daughter. Tell me who she was and what she enjoyed in life. After that I can start sending you some questions to answer and we'll continue down that path until we've uncovered everything.

I look forward to working with you and sincerely hope that this is what will stop those alarming urges plaguing you. Remember, if this starts having the reverse effect, please seek professional help.

Sincerely,
Kody Burkoff

5

"I don't know why she treats me like that," sobbed Mary Jones, the somber-looking, middle-aged woman seated across from me.

Mary, who reminded me of a woman I recently saw on an animal hoarding show, came to me late last week as a referral from a very peculiar psychiatrist in town, Dr. Dunbar. Dr. Dunbar has sent a few clients my way as part of his prescribed treatment. He believes that if his clients can find that one time in their lives when they were the happiest, it will strike a match in them to strive to live for that feeling again. Why Dr. Dunbar didn't help his clients strive for that moment himself was beyond me. I thought that's what they paid him to do. They paid him to help "fix" their problems. Apparently his way of fixing problems involved passing the buck. Regardless, my client list has expanded and I'm still able to pay the bills.

The task at hand was not an easy one, mind you. The people he sent to me were usually severely depressed. They couldn't see the silver lining if it was wrapped around them like a tortilla. Because of patient confidentiality, Dr. Dunbar was unable to clue me in to a client's past. I get it, I really do. No one wants their business broadcast around town. But it would be nice to know which conversations to start and which ones to avoid. For example, I'd like to know that I shouldn't ask about a client's mother or father if the client was severely beaten as a child. I'd also like know that it's best to skip making a fire in my office in the dead of winter if a client is deathly afraid of it and will freak out yelling 911 as she runs down the street. Obviously there were some areas for improvement in our working relationship.

"Mary, it's not you. She's a teenager. Don't you remember being her age? I'll bet you were the same way. We all go through that period in our lives when we think we're better than ninety-nine percent of the adults around us. I know I was a little brat. I did whatever I wanted, basically daring my parents to do something about it. I'm not proud of my actions. I don't think anybody ever really is. Fortunately, most of us grow out of that stage. Not all of us remain self-centered."

I couldn't help but think of a few of my former classmates who didn't grow out of that self-centered stage of life. Becky Flick, for example, has been married three times already and according to her the failed marriages were her husbands' fault. Well, yes, it was their fault for marrying her in the first place, but how can a woman that feels entitled to everything expect to get it from one man? Seems to me what she really needs is a harem so that all of her needs are met at all times, and if a man turns weary, there's always another one to take his place. I guess that's what she's sort of doing anyway. All the men in my hometown are her harem. Eck!

"I've done everything she's ever asked of me. Her father doesn't even know the half of it. He doesn't see what I go through every day." The tears were about to roll so Mary quickly reached for the tissue box. "To him she's still that innocent seven-year-old little girl who colors pictures for his office. When he's at work or wherever else he hides at night, that innocent little girl turns into an evil bitch."

Mary immediately appeared apologetic. "There's no other word to describe her. I try to tell my husband about how she treats me and he turns it around to make it my fault, or her mother's fault. Her mother left her when she was just a baby. I don't know what that woman has to do with anything I'm dealing with on a daily basis."

"I understand what you're saying," I said, trying to be as compassionate as possible, but fully aware that solving this problem was not my expertise. "I think you'll need to take this up with Dr. Dunbar. These issues you have with your stepdaughter are more suitable for your sessions with him." I made a motion to signify a connection between the two of us. "You and I are supposed to be looking back in your life to a time when you felt the happiest. I want to hear about joy and laughter. I want to hear about the time you almost wet yourself from laughing so hard or when you made love in the park and barely escaped the eyes of a passerby. Those are the types of memories you need to conjure up for me. Leave all those day-to-day worries behind when you enter this office. Your job is to come in here fully focused on what made you happy in the past and what will make you happy in the future." I grasped Mary's hand. "Can we do that? Can we focus on Mary Jones' happiness right now?"

Mary still had tears brimming in her eyes, but my encouraging words might have stopped the downpour from occurring. Sometimes I got carried away with my pep talks, but hell if she didn't need one. It was people like her who made me feel so guilty about hating my life some days. I mean, what did I really have to complain about? I was young and healthy. I had a great family and great friends. Of course, the only thing missing was true love. After Kevin and I broke up, I decided to give myself until thirty-five before I sent in for a mail-order-husband. What? There's got to be at least one good-looking Russian man searching for love.

"You're right, Kody. This is not what I'm here to do. I am here to better myself. I am here to seek out my source of pure bliss." Mary took a deep breath. As she exhaled, she said, "I might need a little help."

"Of course. Here." I handed Mary a pad of paper and a pencil. "Why don't we write down our favorite things in life? These are things that bring a smile to our face or leave a good taste in our mouth. Let's just start writing until we run out of ideas and then we can share our thoughts. It's a good way for us to get to know each other too."

Mary and I got started. Knowing exactly what made me happy, I quickly jotted down cookies, brownies, pizza, convertibles, good-looking single men, my family, Kendall, books, mountains, oceans, CSI: Crime Scene Investigation, and the Food Network channel. These items weren't necessarily in order of importance, just the order they popped into my head. If I were to put them in order, there would be a three-way tie between cookies, my family, and Kendall. I couldn't live without any of them. The key was moderation.

I looked over at Mary who was supposed to be furiously writing. She was instead staring mindlessly out the window. My first reaction was irritation that she wasn't trying hard enough. My second reaction was sadness because I quickly remembered why she was here in the first place. Mary had lost her happy place.

Hoping that she had written down at least one item, I asked her to share her list with me.

"Well, I couldn't think of too many things," she said, acting more like a shy child than a mature woman in her late forties. "My mindset isn't quite there yet, I guess. Um…the first thing I have on my list is attending plays. I used to attend quite a few with my mother and sisters." Mary scooted back in her seat. "Geez. That was over ten years ago. I don't tell many people this, but I was very involved in the drama club in high school. I was one of those kids who wore all black and hung out in the theater after school every day even if we weren't working on a production." Sighing heavily, she continued, "Those days seem like they never happened."

"Tell me more," I urged, not wanting her mood to spiral downward again. She obviously had a passion for the theater arts so talking about it just might be the answer we've both been looking for. "Tell me more about your acting roles in high school."

She hesitated, but then continued as requested.

"I was cast as the scarecrow in The *Wizard of Oz* my junior year. The costume was incredibly itchy and I had to practice walking like I was about to fall down, but other than that it was a lot of fun. I, of course, really wanted to be Dorothy. That part went to Celia Brown, the most popular girl in school. She always landed the lead role and I was always jealous of her. Even now, I heard she was president of some big company in Texas. Some people are just born to succeed. I'm still not sure what I was born to do."

Okay. The sulking was already getting old. Maybe Dr. Dunbar had her prescription wrong. "I'm sure you were an amazing scarecrow," I said. "Did you continue acting after high school?"

"I had a few small roles in the community theater, nothing memorable. I lost my confidence after college. I took to sitting in the audience rather than standing on the stage."

"That's too bad."

"Yeah, my mom wished that I had continued too. She loved the theater. When I quit trying out she was devastated. But it wasn't all that bad since that was when we started attending them together. My sisters eventually joined us."

"And you don't do that anymore?"

"Not since my mom died from breast cancer almost ten years ago. My sisters and I don't even get together all that often anymore. And when we do, there's still that void in the room like something is missing."

"I'm sorry to hear about your mom. That must have been hard for you and your family." Hoping for a subject with a happier ending, I asked, "What else is on your list?"

"Babies."

Oh, great. This was probably where she told me she was unable to have children or she had five miscarriages and stopped trying after her doctor told her she was risking her life. I didn't know if I was ready for this.

"I'm unable to have children," Mary said.

Am I good or what?

"I've accepted the fact. It wasn't easy, mind you. I must still have that motherly instinct though because whenever I'm around babies and young children my heart just melts and all my worries fade away. I don't know what it is. I felt like that when my stepdaughter was younger too. Maybe that's why it breaks my heart so much to see what she has grown into. She used to be such a sweet little thing who loved being with me. When I first met my husband, Mark, she followed me around everywhere. I wonder now if I fell more in love with Mark or with Stacy."

Mary sighed, indicating that her thoughts were heading in the wrong direction. Again. She was like a roller coaster with her mood swings, which immediately reminded me of a guy I dated a few years back, subsequently named Mark. Mark was so much fun when he was on top of that giant hill looking down at the crowd below. He was funny, romantic, creative, and spontaneous. When that coaster started to plummet though, so did his attitude. He was argumentative, pouty, sullen, and only negative thoughts streamed out of his mouth. I tried riding the roller coaster with him for a while, but like all good rides, they come to an end. If only I was an amusement park operator, maybe I could have fixed Mark so that he was stuck at the top forever. Oh well, at least now I know that I should be searching for a merry-go-round instead.

"Let's not go there, Mary. What else is on your list?"

"Nothing. I could only think of those two things."

Alrighty then. Not quite sure where to go next with our conversation, I glanced at the time on my laptop. Almost noon. Time to wrap things up. I couldn't help but feel guilty for wanting this session to be over, but Mary was one tough cookie to crack.

"I think you should set up another appointment with Dr. Dunbar before we try this again. I'm not sure you're able to focus on your happiness quite yet."

"I make you feel uncomfortable, don't I?"

Yes, you do, I thought, but instead I said, "Of course not."

"I know I'm hard to talk to. People brush me off all the time. They'll excuse themselves from our conversation and then I'll watch them walk over to someone who isn't so depressing. I go home and cry afterward. I cry because I didn't used to be this way. I used to be happy all the time. I used to smile when my husband and stepdaughter came home from work and school. Now they avoid me too. I feel like everyone avoids me. What happened to me? How did I get this way?"

Mary was no longer sitting on the loveseat across from me. She was instead pacing back and forth squeezing herself as though she might fall apart even more if she let go. This woman definitely needed a hug. It was the least I could do. As I held Mary, her cry elevated to a sob. She shook in my arms. My heart went out to her. Her depression had driven away everyone close to her, and now she had to rely on the help of strangers to get her out of her funk.

While my shoulder soaked up her tears, I thought about how lucky I was to have caring friends and family in my life, all of whom I felt comfortable going to if my life were to fall to pieces. I used to think my life was falling apart every time a relationship failed so I kept them all pretty busy. Now that I was older, I dealt with breakups better. More often than not I blamed the guy for either not seeing what he had with me or for being a complete doofus. Calling them names always made me feel better too.

Mary's sobbing returned to a gentle cry and she finally released her grip on me. I, too, released my grip.

"Are you going to be okay?" I asked.

"I'll be fine. Thank you for your time today. You're a good person, Kody."

With that, Mary was out the door. I should've said more. I should've asked if she wanted me to call someone. I already knew the answer though. She didn't have anyone. She was going home to finish crying alone.

I reached for the phone on my desk to call Dr. Dunbar, readying myself to tell him poor Mary was all his. She needed the help of a doctor, not someone who studied the writings of Shakespeare in college. Plus, he needed to know what happened today.

Something stopped me from pushing that little green button though. If I betrayed Mary's trust by telling Dr. Dunbar that she was his problem and not mine, I'd be doing the same thing everyone else had done to her. I'd be walking away from her. I'd be giving her the cold shoulder. My gut was telling me to give her another chance. She deserved at least that much. She deserved a hell of a lot more, but with the combination of her lack of self-confidence and the disrespect from her husband and stepdaughter, the kindness of a stranger might be like a gift from above. I quickly decided that if Mary had no one, she now had me.

My cell phone began to ring. I reached into the bottom desk drawer for my purse and clumsily swashed my hand through the main compartment until I came up with my prize. It was Brian. Brian was a simple man with a complicated story.

"I'm not interrupting anything, am I?" he asked.

"No. I was just sitting here gathering my thoughts. What's up?"

"I need a favor. A co-worker gave me two tickets to the Twins game on Saturday afternoon and…"

"Brian, I thought we decided you weren't ready to date yet."

He sighed. "Kody, I was going to ask you to watch Anna so I can take Ethan with me. He'll be so excited. He hasn't been to a game yet."

Where was my damn foot when I needed it? How presumptuous of me to assume Brian was going to ask me to go to the game with him. We'd already tried dating. It was a disaster to say the least. His wife, who was once a client of mine, passed away from cancer about six months ago. Neither Brian nor the kids were ready for another woman in their lives just yet. Brian thought he was ready, but our date told him otherwise. Even though we didn't say her name, Amanda was in our thoughts. It was as though she was sitting at the table with us, taking turns eating off our plates.

"Of course, I don't know what I was thinking. Ethan will love it. You two deserve a little guy time. And I don't have any major plans on Saturday so I'd love to hang out with Anna. We can go shopping or do something girly, whatever she wants."

"That's great, Kody. I really appreciate it. I'll get you back. I promise."

"No need for that."

"Yes, I believe there is. You are an amazing woman and my kids and I are truly lucky to have you in our lives."

"Well, thank you."

"You're welcome. Is ten too early?"

"Ten sounds great. I'll see you then."

What a sweet guy with a truly sad story. I'll never forget working with Amanda. Unfortunately, cancer was pretty much eating her alive when I met her. She came to me because she wanted to leave something for her children to remember her by. We were only able to meet a few times so we didn't get too much accomplished. I was even called in to the hospital near the end so that she could record her final messages. It was hard to maintain my composure around her. I had never heard words so moving in all my life. Her strength and compassion has since inspired me to be more open in my relationships. I believe that people come into our lives for a reason and what I've taken from my time with Amanda is that whatever I'm dealt, I need to continue to move forward. Life will happen whether I want it to or not. I might as well make the best of it.

6

To: kodyburkoff@inyourwords.com
From: sad_dad1@gmail.com
Subject: My Julia

I took the liberty of deleting some details from Julia's obituary per our agreement of anonymity.

Julia xxx, 18, of xxx died on xxx at the xxx hospital in xxx.

Julia was born on xxx to sad dad and xxx in xxx. She was active in her high school: volleyball, track, and a member of the student council. Her favorite subject was science because of her desire to find the answers to the most difficult questions. Julia had planned to attend college to study biology. Her dream was to go on to medical school to find a cure for cancer.

Julia's other interests included: watching movies with her mother, driving around town with her father, catching frogs and toads with her brother, gardening with her grandmother, playing Frisbee with her dog, Attaboy, and spending time with her friends.

She also enjoyed the outdoors: skiing, camping, fishing, hiking, and snowshoeing. Julia prided herself on being adventurous and was willing to try anything.

Her spirit for life, positive attitude and genuine love made people of all ages want to be her friend. She will be missed by her family and by all those who knew her.

That was who my daughter was before that monster took her from our lives. Of course, she was more than that. She was beautiful. She smelled of lilacs, which were her favorite flower. She wore a locket around her neck that was given to her by her mother when she was twelve. She wore that locket every day even though her friends made fun of it. Julia didn't care what anyone said. She made her own choices and nothing her friends said made her change her mind. I guess in the end that stubbornness got the best of her.

After Julia was murdered, her friends told the police that they told her not to go off with that boy. They said they had just met him; he had recently moved to town. Julia didn't want to listen to them. She apparently thought it was a good decision to go off with someone she barely knew.

I get so angry when I think about this again, yet a day doesn't go by without me seeing an image of her falling to the ground, her body lifeless. I get angry with Julia for being so stubborn and stupid. I get even angrier with that boy who took her life. He told the police that while he was holding her in his arms he tripped over a tent rope and Julia's head struck a metal stake that was sticking out of the ground. I can't accept the police report. I have it in my head that he had more to do with it. He pushed her or tripped her. For some reason my mind wants to keep coming up with stories for what might really be the truth.

Do you understand why I need your help? According to the police, the boy, and a few buzzed witnesses, my lovely daughter died spiraling in the arms of her suitor. I wasn't there though. They might all be covering for the kid. Maybe he was dragging her off to his tent so that he could rape her. Maybe he drugged her and she stumbled because she was so impaired. Maybe she was fighting him off as they got closer to his tent and she pushed herself away only to fall and hit her head. I could go on and on. All it comes down to now is that my daughter is dead and the boy who knows the truth is living and breathing. The general public believes his story. They even feel sorry for him. They say it wasn't his fault. Well, it sure as hell wasn't my fault. He's the only one I have to blame.

Sincerely,
sad dad

7

The obituary was a nice touch—a very direct insight into how sad dad still saw his daughter. Even after almost a year, he was incredibly fixated on her death instead of on the life that he was fortunate enough to share with her. That was the first thing I needed to change if this was going to work.

As I began typing a response, I heard a faint whistling sound coming from outside. I looked out the front window and saw Charlie strolling down the sidewalk with what appeared to be a skip in his step. This must be a happy day.

"Good morning, Kody. Beautiful day, isn't it?" he said as I opened the door for him.

"Why, yes it is. What's got you in such a good mood this morning?" I asked, motioning for him to join me at the small table near the front windows. I was feeling the need to soak up some early morning sunshine. It also might help Charlie stick with his sunny disposition.

Charlie was an especially perplexing guy. One day he was happy about life, telling me how wonderful his childhood was. The next time we met he would rant about how his father beat him if he didn't do his chores exactly right, or about how his brother made fun of his large ears. I didn't notice that his ears were larger in size than anyone else's, but we all held a hatred for at least one of our body parts.

I, too, have always had a complex about my ears. My brother knew that was my sore spot, so to speak. Anytime I was feeling good about myself, he said either, "Hey, Dumbo!" or "Can you make those things flap?" His words made me so angry, partly because I believed he was telling the truth and partly because I let him get to me. That look of satisfaction on his face was enough to make me go in his room and rip something up. That's what I did back then. I ripped up his homework, pictures of his girlfriend, and his favorite sports trading cards. Fortunately, he's grown into a decent enough guy and I've grown into my ears and out of that bad habit.

As for Charlie, I had thought about making him wear one of those mood rings that were such a hit in middle school. Everyone had one. I only remember mine looking black, which I looked up the meaning of not too long ago. One website said black meant stressed, nervous, and tense. Knowing that made me wonder if mine was really working at the time, although I did pick it up from a gumball machine. Stressed and tense really didn't fit my personality, especially back then. I look back on those years with such happiness. I was on top of the world. It wasn't until after middle school, when puberty hit me like a Mack truck that I felt stressed, nervous, and tense. Yes, I already mentioned I was a late bloomer. Remember the middle school dance story?

"My lady friend cooked me a marvelous breakfast after a marvelous evening. I didn't get much sleep last night, if you know what I mean," he said with a smirk and devilish raise of the eyebrows.

Good thing I only had coffee for breakfast this morning because I'm pretty sure I would have lost it about now. I hated hearing about people my parents' age having sex. It always conjured up really bad visuals. Yes, I realize everyone has sex, including my parents, but that is *not* something I like to think about. No one does. It also didn't help that Charlie was moderately overweight and sported a comb over.

Try picturing a naked hillbilly version of Donald Trump and tell me your stomach doesn't churn.

"Okay. Let's get started, shall we?" I said, hoping he didn't feel it necessary to disclose any more details about his night of lust.

"Ready when you are."

"We left off with you telling me that you met your second wife at the casino. She was sitting next to you at the nickel slot machines."

"Yep. Neither of us was having much luck that night until I hit three cherries in a row and won five hundred dollars. I jumped around with my fists in the air, hooting and hollering. I suppose I made quite a scene, but I had never won that much money before. I haven't won that much money since then either. While I waited for the cashier to come over and hand me my winnings, I noticed Catherine, who was sitting next to me, looking as disappointed as a kid who'd just lost her balloon. She later confessed that she was incredibly jealous. She had been sitting in my stool for quite some time before finally switching machines only minutes before I sat down."

"She must have been frustrated. Is that when you started a conversation with her?"

Charlie smiled broadly as he continued. "I asked her if she wanted to join me for dinner. She was a good-looking woman, blond though, not brunette like I prefer. Catherine was also the closest woman to me and I was in the mood to celebrate. With only a little hesitation, she accepted my offer. I'm glad she did too because that night turned out to be one of the best I ever had. We ate dinner, gambled, listened to live music, danced, and made out in the back seat of a taxi cab."

"You're quite the ladies' man."

Patting his protruding belly, he said, "I was about fifty pounds lighter back then. Not to brag, but I was quite a catch."

"I'm sure you were," I grinned. "Looking back, do you think it was love at first sight?"

"Nah. I wouldn't go that far. Like I said, I prefer brunettes. I grew to love her as I'm sure she did me."

Before asking my next question about their relationship, the front door slammed open like a pack of kids entering a Chuck E. Cheese's. A confident-looking man about my age sauntered into the room not bothering to close the door behind him.

"Pardon my intrusion, but I'm looking for the owner of this establishment," he said as he walked over to the table Charlie and I were seated around.

"You found her," I said, standing up to shake his outstretched hand.

Charlie stood to shake his hand as well.

"My name is Sam Snyder. I'm moving in next door so I thought it only appropriate to come over and introduce myself. I'm a financial planner. I'll be offering a whole slew of services once the construction is done, which I hope will be at the end of next week. Things aren't moving along quite as fast as I'd like them to. I swear those guys take more coffee breaks than my grandmother."

Sam's eyes scoured me from head to toe. Could he be any more obvious?

"And who might you be?" he finally asked.

"I'm Kody Burkoff." I motioned to Charlie. "This is Charlie, one of my clients. We're working on his memoir this morning."

"Ah. I heard that's what was going on over here. Maybe I'll have to have you document my success story when I strike it rich."

"I'm sure we could work something out, Mr. Snyder."

"Please, call me Sam."

"Okay, Sam. Are you moving from another office in town?"

"Yeah. I was with Simpson and Reed for almost two years. I got tired of all their company policies so I up and left to start my own business. It's always been a dream of mine; to be successful and have done it all on my own. It might sound pompous to others, but I have to look out for number one, you know what I mean?"

"I think so."

"You married?" he asked, abruptly.

"No."

"Engaged?"

"No."

"Serious with anyone?"

"No."

"You might want to ask me out sometime. I might say yes," he said, licking his lips.

Oh, no. He did *not* just do that. I looked over at Charlie who was working hard to stifle his laughter. Extending my hand and forcing a fake smile, I said, "It was very nice to meet you. Charlie and I should really get back to his memoir before he needs to leave for work."

Charlie took my hint and motioned to the open door.

With his tongue back in his mouth, Sam said, "I understand. Time is money. Be sure to stop by when you're not busy and we'll go over your portfolio. I won't even charge you being that we're neighbors and all."

"I'll keep that in mind."

"It was nice meeting you, Kody. You too, Charlie."

After Sam left, Charlie winked and said, "Eligible bachelor next door and I think he's interested."

"He's disgusting. Did you see the way he licked his lips at me? He's totally not my type."

Charlie laughed. I couldn't help but join him. Maybe having a new neighbor wasn't going to be that great after all.

"Let's stick to your love life, shall we?" I said.

"Okay, but you should keep him in mind. He said so himself that he plans to strike it rich. He might be a keeper."

"He might be a loser. Now, tell me about your marriage to your second wife."

Settling back in and wiping the smirk off his face, Charlie continued where he left off. "Catherine basically moved in with me the day after we met and we were married a month later. Our quick nuptials surprised our family and friends, but when we weren't at work we spent every waking moment together. We were just having so much fun. We didn't see any reason to wait."

Charlie went on to describe the details of their Las Vegas wedding. I couldn't have recommended a better location for a couple that met at a casino. I took notes, but I also thought about my friend, and former client, Nancy, whom I hadn't seen in a few weeks. She lived in Las Vegas for almost twenty years before leaving to start a new chapter of her life in the Midwest. We met for lunch regularly to work on her memoir and ultimately became good friends despite our incredibly different pasts.

"Sounds like the perfect wedding. You two must have been very happy."

"We were. We were truly happy for about a year. But because we hadn't taken the time to get to know each other properly, I didn't find out until after we were married that Catherine was a kleptomaniac."

I didn't see that coming.

"She's in jail for stealing. I'm a poster child for long-term relationships, or else it's the other way around. I don't know."

The now sullen Charlie sat across from me with no more wind left in his sail. I should have left well enough alone, but because I was a curious person when it came to situations like these, I had to ask how he found out about his wife's compulsion.

"The first indication was when we went to a friend's house and the wife caught Catherine loading up her purse with fridge magnets of all things. Come to find out these weren't the first things she had stolen from dinner parties. When it finally came out in our circle of friends, they had put the blame on Catherine for many items that they claimed went missing. I didn't know what the real story was because Catherine never came clean with any of it. It wasn't until I found her secret stash in our house that I finally understood the seriousness of her problem. The two drawers of her nightstand were stuffed full with medications, jewelry, makeup, trinkets, dog toys, and you name it. I think she got away with it for so long because the items she chose to steal were small. They were things that she could stow away in her purse."

"I'm so sorry to hear that. Was finding all those items what ended your marriage?" I asked.

"No. We tried marriage counseling, and then she tried counseling on her own. In the end, she was too ashamed of her behavior that she couldn't stand to be around me, and certainly not our friends. One day she just left. I only know she's in jail because I have a buddy that works at the state prison." Charlie glanced at his watch. It was nearing the nine o'clock hour. "I better get to work," he said, pushing himself away from the table. His gaze lingered on the woman walking by. "I'll see you next week sometime. I'll give you a call."

I hated for him to leave so unhappy after arriving high on life. He must have been heartbroken when Catherine left him. Unfortunately, Charlie was no stranger to this type of behavior from women. His first wife ran off with a married man from her office. After a one-year torrid affair, the two adulterers left their spouses and moved to Rapid City, South Dakota. Charlie said he never saw it coming.

Unrequited love. The worst kind of all.

I knew somewhat how Charlie was feeling. I had been infatuated with a few guys in my time, nothing close to being considered love, mind you. But as fate would have it, they just weren't all that interested in me. Go figure. The hot instructor from the gym was one of them, or is one of them I should say. He's buff, beautiful, and has the nicest ass I've ever seen. This is horrible of me, but I always jump on a treadmill behind him when he's running. I can't help but stare. I don't even know if he's the total package yet. You know, body *and* brains. I've never actually held a real conversation with him. We'll exchange hellos when passing each other on our way to another machine, or say, "That was a great workout," after a kickboxing class. Part of me doesn't even want to get to know him. My whole fantasy might be ruined if he turns out to be a total Neanderthal. For all I know, he's married with five kids from five different women. Whatever. It's one fantasy I'm willing to hang on to.

8

To: sad_dad1@gmail.com
From: kodyburkoff@inyourwords.com
Subject: Baby Julia

Dear sad dad,

Let's take a step back eighteen years to remember a tiny, little girl just being born. She's pink with skinny arms and legs floundering in the newfound freedom. Her cry is louder than you ever imagined. Your wife is lying there completely exhausted. She needs to rest. The nurse hands you your precious baby girl. Tears begin to gather in the corner of your eyes. You stare at this new life form for several minutes before uncovering her delicate fingers to make sure they're as beautiful as her mother's. Next, you count the toes. She seems to be complete. It's then that you realize she's yours and you already know you love her.

Tell me how it felt to be a new father. Tell me about the first time Julia said "da da" and meant it. Tell me about the discoveries you and her made together in the backyard. These are the memories that should be included in your memoir. These are the memories of fatherhood, unconditional love, and absolute happiness. I need you to focus on the wonderful moments you shared with your daughter, not her tragic ending. She wouldn't want to be remembered that way. You wouldn't want to be remembered that way.

Your assignment is to write about special memories you have from the first five years of your daughter's life.

Good luck,
Kody

9

"You never called to tell me what you decided to do with that weird e-mail you received. What's up with that?" Kendall asked.

She wasn't one to start a conversation with hello. She usually got right to the point. I, too, had a bone to pick with her, which was why I answered her question with a question.

"What's up with you not telling me you gave my number to Nick?"

Apparently this was the week for old high school boyfriends to reenter my life, although Nick wasn't exactly a boyfriend. He wanted to be my boyfriend. He just didn't have what it took to make the cut.

"Forgot," Kendall said without remorse.

"You don't forget stuff like that."

"I know. Jason did it. I told him he shouldn't interfere with your love life, but he said Nick was really persistent. Did you know he had a crush on you in high school?"

"Jason did? I had no idea," I said sarcastically.

"Very funny."

"Yeah, I sort of figured Nick had a thing for me. He followed me around occasionally asking dumb questions. Does he still have that huge mole on his neck? I couldn't stop staring at it when he talked to me."

"I do remember that now that you mention it. I always felt like it was staring at me. Jason didn't say anything about it so he might've got it removed."

"Or knowing your observant husband, he just didn't notice it."

"Good point. Can we stop talking about large moles so you can tell me about the ax murderer you're now e-mail buddies with?"

"How did you know?"

"I know you, Kody. You're a pushover for helping those that can't be helped. It's in your genes or something. Your mom is that way too. She's always doing odd favors for people."

"Just to clarify, sad dad hasn't committed a crime yet. I gave him the assignment of writing about his daughter from birth to age five. I'm hoping to get him to focus on the time he shared with her while she was still alive. It'll be interesting to read what he writes."

"Well, when the shit hits the fan, I'll be ready to say I told you so."

"I wouldn't expect anything different."

"So, are you going to give Nick a chance?"

"I doubt it. I wasn't interested then so why would I be now?"

Even though I couldn't see Kendall, I knew her eyes were rolling to the back of her head. It was true though. Why would I like him now if I didn't like him then? I had the same philosophy toward all those mean and snooty girls in high school. I had no intention of ever befriending them no matter how much I heard from other people that they were really nice now. I had scars, people, mental scars. Under no circumstance was I going to open my heart to someone who made me feel so inferior.

"People change, Kody. You've changed. You should really…"

"Gotta go, Kendall. Someone's at the door. I'll give you a call later," I said before hanging up. I would hear about that later.

Not wanting to think about high school and the drama that went with it, I settled in to do some work. Brainstorming ways to communicate with Mary Jones was on the top of my list. I couldn't have her coming in here sucking all the positive energy from the room when she came back.

Savoring the flavor and caffeine of my diet cola, I noticed a boy of about ten or eleven pass slowly by my door. Even though it was July and kids were riding bike past all the time, I didn't often see them loitering out front. There wasn't anything for a kid to do around here. When the boy passed by a third time, I figured that was my queue to intervene.

"Are you looking for someone?" I asked.

Rather shyly, the boy said, "I'm looking for the ghostwriter. That's you, right?"

"That's me. What can I do for you?"

Looking around as though he didn't want anyone to see us talking, he asked if we could go inside. I opened the door and followed him in.

"You might think this is weird," he started and then paused to look around the office, "but I'm pretty sure that I'm going to die this year. We're all going to die. You too."

I didn't know how to respond. I had no idea a boy this age could be so serious *and* have the guts to come in here to tell me I was going to die.

"How can you be so sure?" I asked, playing along. I couldn't wait to hear what he had to say. The kid looked normal enough, but I had read some crazy stories on the Internet recently.

"I believe there is going to be a zombie apocalypse. Zombies will take over the world. Well, actually they'll end the world by roaming the streets eating all the living creatures until there's nothing left to devour. It's pretty scary stuff."

I nodded my head, looking as sincerely concerned as possible. "It sounds scary. What's your name? Do your parents know you're here?"

"My name is Alex. No, I can't tell my parents I'm here. They don't believe in zombies. They don't think it can really happen, at least not in their lifetime. I watched a show about it the other night and it's all over the Internet. Check it out. Google zombie apocalypse and start reading."

"I hate to tell you this, Alex, but I'm not sure I believe in zombies either."

"Haven't you seen any scary movies? How do think the movie makers came up with the idea for zombies? Somebody somewhere saw one."

Alex seemed so determined to persuade me that his zombie theory was correct even though he still hadn't told me why he was here or how he perceived me being involved.

"Here," I said, setting my laptop in front of him, "show me what you're talking about."

If it was one thing I knew about kids, it was that they were persistent. Alex wanted to believe what he read and there was nothing I was going to say to change his mind. He quickly pulled up the website that was feeding his fears and turned the machine toward me. I skimmed the page, shocked by what I was reading: how to prepare a survival kit, how to make an emergency plan, and what weapons were best to have on hand in case of a zombie attack.

"Well, I can see how all this stuff might frighten you. Where does it say that it's going to happen this year?" I asked.

Alex took control of the machine once again and scrolled down the page. "Here. *Zombie245* says 'the end is soon.' I took that to mean by the end of the year."

"Alex, that is just someone's blog post. You can't go by what he or she says."

"I'm not!" he said, getting visibly upset. It was safe to assume he received the same reaction from his parents or some other adult. "I think it will happen soon too. I just have this feeling."

I was left speechless. How do you argue with his feeling? I had certain hunches about things too. Not about zombies barging into my house wanting to eat my brain though.

"Um…well…I can't say that I agree with you. I mean, a lot of things *might* happen. We *might* have a huge earthquake where the planet splits in two, the sun *might* explode tomorrow, or a huge sinkhole *might* appear and suck us all to the center of the earth where we'll boil like a giant pot of stew."

"You're just like my parents and every other adult I've talked to. I don't get it. I thought you might be different."

"I'm sorry, Alex."

"I'm out of here," he said, being true to his word. He threw the door open and sprinted down the sidewalk. I stood holding the door staring after him. Never in a million years would I have guessed that I was going to have that conversation today. Zombies? A zombie apocalypse no less? Yet another good reason not to rush into a relationship and have children. I should wait until the apocalypse is over first.

Refocusing my attention on the living, I glanced at the clock. It was almost time to meet up with my gardening club. Don't laugh. Creating a killer garden wasn't exactly at the top of my bucket list, but it was something I had always wanted to be successful at. I really enjoyed learning gardening tips and tricks from the other women in the group. I only caught a little grief once in a while, usually when Kendall was feeling sassy. She would ask me, "Aren't you a little young to be hanging out with the senior citizen group?" I either ignored her or said something sassy back like, "Doesn't it get old hanging out with the soccer moms?" That usually shut her right up. She *did not* like to be grouped with the soccer moms for whatever reason.

The gardening gals, our self-proclaimed nickname, also had a lot of great stories to share, besides about gardening. Because the majority of the members were over sixty-five, they had lived a lot of life and didn't hold back when it came to spilling personal anecdotes. The best part of all, most of them didn't care that I was still single. By now, they were downright tired of their husbands and were glad for an excuse to get out of the house. I was the envy of the crowd. I had no one to cook and clean for. I did anything I wanted to without guilt. They made being single sound almost glamorous. I didn't have the heart to tell them that it wasn't as great as it sounded. Being single meant that for the most part I ate alone, every meal. I didn't have someone to guilt into going shopping with me. I also didn't have someone to rub my back when I learned of some bad news. Maybe their husbands didn't do much around the house or they wouldn't go dancing on Saturday night, but those women knew that their husbands loved them very much and would do anything for them. A lot can be said for that lump on the couch.

I was the last to arrive at our gardening plot. When I pulled up, the gals were tending to their own sections of the land, checking for signs of damage from weather or wildlife, and measuring each plant's growth. The plot, donated to us by a retired farmer, was located just outside of town next to a wooded area. This location required us to build fences to keep out the deer and other animals that lived next door. For the most part we didn't have any trouble, but every once in a while an animal found an entry point to wreak havoc on our crops. We then had to spend our gardening time repairing the fence while listening to some of the women tell related stories of destruction.

"Not one for being early, huh, Kody?" Marjie, a fellow gardening gal, asked sarcastically while she picked raspberries, popping every other one into her mouth. "The rest of us have been here for almost an hour already."

"When did you actually get your hands dirty though?" I asked, knowing that they met earlier for coffee and goodies.

"Well, you know us," she said, batting her hand at me. "You need to try Helen's bars. She really outdid herself this week."

"I'll get to it. I need to check on my tomatoes first. I have to make sure they're bigger than yours," I said with a smirk.

"You sound just like my Harold."

I left Marjie to her raspberries and wandered off to check on my garden. Everything appeared to be prospering rather well. I even thought my tomatoes were bigger than Marjie's, not that I wanted to brag. As I marveled at the vines heavy with sugar snap peas, I heard a scream. It was a blood-curdling scream like you would hear in the movies. I stood up to look for the source and saw a sea of white hair moving in one direction. I did the same, only faster. I was first to arrive at the scene.

"What's wrong, Helen?" I asked. "Did you see something? Was there a snake?"

Helen didn't answer. She was in a state of shock. Thinking there might be an animal hiding out in her vegetables, I quickly led her to the grassy area where we sat for coffee. By now, the rest of the women were surrounding us frantically asking questions. Finally, Helen gestured back toward her garden.

"Is something in there?" I asked.

"Did you see a mouse, Helen?" Marjie asked.

Helen remained speechless.

"Damn it, Helen! Did you lose your teeth? You need to say something," shouted Bobbi, a gardening gal not known for her tact.

"There's a girly magazine in my corn! It's the same one Jimmy used to read." Helen brought her hands to her face and broke down in tears.

Silence fell over the group.

In a whisper, Marjie informed me that Helen's husband, Jimmy, passed away about a year ago. This explained why Helen was so distraught over her discovery. I could only imagine what she was thinking. Had Jimmy's spirit returned? Did he leave his magazine behind to send Helen a message? Sort of an odd way to tell someone you're still thinking of them. Men did think differently though.

I squeezed Helen tighter and told her what she needed to hear, "Everything will be okay. We'll get rid of the magazine."

"No!" she said with a note of panic. "I want to keep it. Jimmy must have wanted me to have it."

"Sure. No problem," I said. "We'll go get it for you."

Very slowly, as if Jimmy might jump out from the chest-high corn at any second, the ladies huddled together and crept over to Helen's garden plot to snag the magazine. They argued over who was actually going to touch it.

I couldn't help but wonder how the magazine had really got into Helen's corn. Maybe a group of teenage boys came out here to escape the eyes of the town and threw it away when they were finished ogling over the pictures. Maybe it blew in through the fence somehow. Or maybe the farmer who donated this land came out here to page through the magazine in peace. It wasn't my place to say anything, especially since Helen appeared to like the idea that her Jimmy was sending her a message. Her favorite flower might have been a better choice.

With the magazine safely in Helen's hands, we made the unanimous decision to finish off the rest of the food and coffee the other women had brought. This gave me the perfect opportunity to ask them if they had knowledge of an accident last summer where a teenage girl was killed. Their responses were less than helpful.

"I don't know anything about that. My husband thinks it's a waste of time to read the paper."

"I think I heard something about that, but I'm not sure. All those murders run together."

"My cousin's son committed a murder some years ago. He's still in jail, you know. That boy ripped that poor family apart. Such a shame."

"Oh, well, my great-grandfather murdered his neighbor for trying to steal a cow. As it turned out, it was the neighbor's cow to begin with. That's how my mother used to tell the story."

"I watch the news every morning, but only on *Fox*. I can't wait to get those damn liberals out of office."

Alrighty then.

"So, none of you remember a young, high school girl getting killed last summer? Her name was Julia. It was ruled an accident, but it seems to me this sort of story would have had coverage on the television or in the newspaper."

The women all shook their heads. Unbelievable. If they hadn't heard of sad dad's daughter, then I knew for a fact he didn't live in town or within a thirty mile radius. In these parts, gossip kept a town alive. What else did people talk about? It's not like these women kept up with the Kardashians. Or did they?

While the women continued to compare murder stories, I wandered off to pull weeds in my garden. I didn't have any good stories to share. Not yet anyway. Maybe one of these days I could share the story of how I stopped a murder from happening, or if Kendall was correct, the story of how I tried, but failed.

10

I look at her baby pictures and see blood. I see her bleeding in the exact spot where her head struck the metal stake. Her death is all I think about, especially today. It's my little angel's birthday. She would have been nineteen years old and home from college for the summer. I would have got her a job helping out at the school. They always need good kids as role models. She was the perfect role model. Was. I hate that word. She WAS murdered. She WAS taken from this world. She WAS taken from my life.

I'll try to stick to my assignment, which is to focus on the life we shared, not her unfortunate death. Remembering her birthdays is how I'll do that.

When Julia turned one she was already walking. She was saying a few words too, one of which was "da da." Having your own flesh and blood recognize you as a father cannot be described in words. I think I glowed every time I heard her say it. She would look at

53

me with those big, blue eyes, say "da da" and hand me something that she needed help with. She needed me. I needed her. I needed her unconditional love. She never judged me like I'm being judged these days. They don't think I see their stares, but I do. Everyone in the old neighborhood thinks I'm crazy. They think that's why Gina and I split up. Gina kicked me out. She said I was too angry. I have every right to be angry. My daughter's murderer is walking around enjoying his privileged life.

Julia's second birthday party was at our neighborhood park. There were a few other families with kids her age that lived close by so we let them all play together while we sat around talking about kid stuff. Well, the moms talked about kid stuff. Us dads tried to show our manhood by discussing sports. It was tough in that setting: pink and purple balloons adorning each table, a princess cake surrounded by gifts, and little ears everywhere. One can't always talk about the Twins without a few cuss words. We all had a good time though. It was for Julia, my little girl. I would have done anything for her. I would still do anything for her. That's why I won't let him get away with it. I won't let him get away with killing my daughter.

Birthday number three was a family affair. Gina wasn't feeling well. She was pregnant with our second child then and had a lot of complications. Fortunately, our son, Gabe, was born without complications. With the birth of a son, our family was complete. We had it all. Looking back, life was so simple then compared to when Julia entered her teens. We didn't worry about any outside influences. What we said was the rule. The competition with friends, coaches, and teachers hadn't been part of the picture yet.

Not to get off topic, but Julia's death hit Gabe especially hard. He and Julia were best buds. He still called her, Joojie, the name he used when he was a toddler. After Julia passed, Gina, not wanting to lose another child, focused all of her attention on Gabe. She was able to move on probably because of that. She even forgave Julia's killer. That's another reason why our marriage didn't last. I haven't been able to move forward like she has and I most certainly will never forgive that little bastard.

I didn't react the same way Gina did when it came to Gabe. The two of us have never been real close. We've yet to find a hobby or an event that entertains us both. I've tried every technique I learned while earning my teaching degree to create some sort of bond with him. He's always preferred the attention of his mother. Gina told me to leave him alone, that someday he and I might find something to do together. I thought having a son was going to be great. I'd always envisioned us going to baseball games together or spending mornings on the lake fishing for bass. Yet another disappointment.

Gina still calls me once a week to see how I'm doing. She says she didn't leave because she stopped loving me. She says it's because I scare her. She's scared that I'll do something stupid like commit murder. I haven't told her that's why I'm talking to you. You said you would help me.

You can picture how birthdays four and five went. I know you don't have kids, but I don't doubt you celebrate birthdays with Kendall's kids.

Sincerely,
sad dad

11

I was in trouble now. He knew who I was. He knew Kendall and I were friends. Kendall was going to kill me!

This could not have turned out worse. Now I would be looking over my shoulder everywhere I went. Every man in his forties would be under suspicion, assuming he wasn't one of those parents who waited until later in life to have children, in which case I needed to extend my suspicion to men in their fifties. That was a big chunk of the male species to look out for. Fortunately, I really didn't get out much these days. Even so, this guy probably knew where to find me.

Besides feeling completely vulnerable about having sad dad know so much about me, I was also boggled by never having heard about his daughter's accident. Everyone knew everyone else's business around here. Well, apparently not everyone. Kendall and I must have been under a rock at the time or, oh, wait a minute. It was probably when we were all at Kendall's parents' cabin for two weeks last summer. That had to be it. Then again, he could have easily conducted an Internet search on me. Who knows what's out there. Or maybe he was a friend of a friend. That was easier to swallow. The last thing I needed was a cyber stalker.

Mary, who was right on time for her appointment, interrupted my thoughts.

"Hi, Kody. This is the right time, isn't it?"

"Yes. Here's your name on my calendar," I said, pointing to her name written on my over-sized desk calendar. "Go on back while I grab what I need." I unplugged my laptop and reached for my water bottle. "Do you need anything to drink? I keep a bottle of whiskey in the cupboard if you're at all interested."

"Do you really?" Mary asked, surprised.

"Sure. Some people need a drink to loosen up. As you know, it isn't always easy to talk about the past."

"Don't I know it. I'm fine for now though. I'll keep it in mind."

Mary walked to the back and sat down on the edge of the loveseat. She folded her hands neatly in her lap; her eyes scanned the works of art I had accumulated over the years from local artists. I held back for a moment to read her body language, trying to uncover the woman beneath the blanket of sadness. Her shoulders were slumped. Her knees were pressed tightly together while her toes turned inward. The clothes she wore were only meant to cover, or hide, her body. Her hair showed too much gray, in my opinion, for a woman her age, and her face was left bare for all to see how the years had taken their toll.

She had the potential to be a beautiful woman. Undoubtedly, she had been beautiful at one time. I bet at one time *she* even thought she was beautiful. The cloud of self-pity surrounding her seemed to weigh her down though. How was I going to rattle up enough positive energy to send that cloud on its way?

Getting settled, I asked, "How would you like to start today?"

"I don't know."

"Do you want to tell me more about your theater days?"

"I don't know."

"Do you want to create another list of items that make you happy?"

"I don't know."

"Hmm," was the only sound I dared to murmur.

I didn't know what else to say. That's not true. I did know what to say. However, what I wanted to say was probably going to set her off and I wasn't sure I wanted to mop up the mess. Her sobbing the other day was already more than I could handle. I didn't want to be completely insensitive because I knew her husband and stepdaughter already had that covered, but I also didn't want to enable this self-pitying behavior.

We sat in silence.

I stared at Mary while she pushed back her cuticles with her fingernails. She was clearly avoiding me. I had never had a client show up refusing to speak. Then I witnessed the first tear splash down onto her hand. I could hold back no longer. Mary needed to hear what I had to say.

"You are the reason you are unhappy," I said stone-faced.

She sat up straight. "What do you mean?"

"I mean, you are in control of your physical and emotional well-being. Your husband and stepdaughter have nothing to do with how you feel about yourself."

"But they treat me so horribly that I can't help but to believe all those awful things they say."

"That's their problem. Not yours. You have to believe that you are a worthwhile human being, that you have the same right as them to live a healthy and happy life. You have to love yourself. Do you love yourself, Mary?"

"Sometimes," she said, covering her eyes.

"That's not good enough. If you don't love yourself, how can you expect anyone else to love you?" I got up to sit next to her on the loveseat. A little human contact never hurt anyone.

"I hate them for making me feel this way," she whispered.

"Forget about them," I replied. "They aren't your immediate problem. You need to fix you first. You need to find the Mary that you love, the one that makes you proud. Somewhere inside is a strong woman that doesn't take shit from anybody."

Oftentimes the truth was harder to hear than the lies. And oftentimes our lies benefitted no one.

Still feeling inspired, I continued my rant. "I know I'm being brutally honest with you, but you need to hear it. When you asked me the other day if you made me uncomfortable, I lied to you. You did make me uncomfortable."

"I figured as much," she said glumly.

"So what are you going to do about it? You have over half your life left. I certainly hope you don't choose to live out your years as miserable as you are now."

"What if I can't find her? What if that woman never comes back?" Mary asked.

"What if…"

What if nothing. My new neighbor was standing in the doorway. Obviously I needed to reinstall the annoying chime on the door.

"Beautiful day out there," Sam said, walking toward us.

Mary hiccupped.

"Why are a couple of hot babes like you hiding in here?"

Mary and I exchanged glances.

"By the looks of it, there's some mama drama going on."

Hot babes. Mama drama.

"Sam, is it?" I asked, knowing full well what his name was. I wanted to pull his ego down just a smidge.

"Yeah, babe. How could you forget a guy like me?"

Ignoring the second babe comment and his question, I said, "We're sort of in the middle of something important. Did you need something?"

"Just wanted to invite you to the grand opening party I'm having tomorrow night at Harry's. Bring a friend. Bring ten if they all look like her," he said, winking at Mary.

Gag me.

Mary smiled broadly. You would have thought she won the lottery. So that's what it took for her to smile, a male chauvinist pig shelling out outrageous compliments. It was good for her self-esteem

I had to admit. I, on the other hand, was more than a little offended. I had known guys like him before, the macho type that still brought their laundry home to their mom. They were all show with not much else to offer. Plus, he was short. There, I said it. He was five feet four with shoes on. Not much taller than the Emerald City munchkins.

At this point, I was on my feet marching toward the door, calculating whether it was big enough to fit his head through. Sam matched my strides, stopping me before my hand could touch the handle.

"You'll come then?" he asked.

Stupid or gutsy, I couldn't tell.

"I'll think about it," I said, biting my tongue.

Nudging my bicep with his shoulder, he said, "We need to get to know each other since we'll be neighbors. You lean on me, I lean *hard* on you."

That did it.

"You need to leave," I said. I figured the look in my eyes spoke the other short-vowel words I would have said if a client wasn't in the room.

Appearing to partially get the message, he opened the door himself. "I'll see you tomorrow," he said with a toothy grin.

When the door closed behind Sam, I said to Mary, "Can you believe the nerve of that guy?"

"I thought he was cute," she said, still smiling.

I shook my head and ushered her back to our seats apologizing for the rude interruption.

"I don't even know where to pick up," I said.

"You were telling me how uncomfortable I made you feel when I was here last."

"Right," I said, feeling a bit awkward. I thought our conversation had gone beyond that. "Did you understand what I meant when I said that?"

"I get it, Kody. You're right. I don't like who I am right now. I don't like the extra weight I've put on," she said, slapping her hips. "I don't like the baggy clothes I wear because of it. My wrinkles are getting deeper and my boobs are sagging lower." Mary took a deep breath. "I don't know how to start loving myself again."

A frown replaced her smile from only seconds ago.

That's when it hit me. "Stop," I said rather sternly. "I have an idea."

Nancy. My ex-Las Vegas showgirl friend, Nancy, was the answer to Mary's problems. Nancy exuded physical beauty, but like Mary, she struggled with acceptance, or rather, allowing others to accept her and the path that she has chosen. These two women seemed an unlikely match, but so were Hugh Hefner and his long string of blonde bimbos. Sometimes people fulfilled each other's needs, regardless of age or sex.

* * * *

"You really think I can help her?" Nancy asked.

Nancy was ecstatic when I asked her to meet me for dinner. We had become good friends since I helped her write her memoir the previous winter. Writing her memoir was a way for her to close the chapter on her past, which included stripping and dancing topless in Las Vegas. She came to Belmont to begin a new, more family-oriented life. Even though she was born and raised in South Dakota, the lifestyle transition was a difficult one. She was making strides, especially with her siblings. She met with them regularly and they were all moving past the void she had created when she left after their parents died.

"I really think she has promise. I mean, don't get me wrong, she needs some work. It's nothing you can't fix. Whatever you can do on the outside is going to make her insides feel better by one hundred percent."

"It's so kind of you to want to help her. I'd love to meet her and see what I can do." Nancy sipped her wine. "Paying it forward. All the love and support you showed me when I first moved here will be paid forward to Mary. If it hadn't been for you, I'd still be stuck in my uncle's basement."

"I highly doubt that. You were born to be in the spotlight. Someone as bright and beautiful as you can't go into hiding for too long."

"You're probably right," she said, batting her long eyelashes.

Our dinner arrived. I ordered broiled salmon with wild rice and sautéed vegetables. Nancy ordered a garden salad with dressing on the side. She still ate like she had to take the stage each night. Our conversation during dinner was what you would expect from two friends who hadn't seen each other in a while: work, family, exercise, and dating. The dating topic took on a life of its own as you can imagine with two single women.

Nancy, who recently turned forty and has never been married, was on the hunt for a man to spend the rest of her life with. I, too, was on the hunt, but that was where our similarities ended. She dated anyone. She didn't care if they owned a mansion or lived in their car. When I asked her why she didn't narrow her scope, she answered, "I don't want to miss out on a good one." I, on the other hand, judged a book by its cover and did not date anyone who did not meet my high standards.

Greg, for example, had it all when it came to earning potential and genuine likeability. His family was normal. He drove a nice car and owned his own home. He was really interested in me, calling every weekend to invite me to dinner or attend an event. I always declined his offers because there was one small item that Greg was missing. He didn't have a chin. No chin. I don't know where it went. Did he ever have one? Did he simply grow out of it? Did he have it removed for health reasons? I was completely stumped. The cover of his book lacked a chin; therefore, Greg lacked the qualifications to have a date with me. Pretty hard core, I know. If it's not right though, it's not right.

"You should try it," Nancy said.

"Try what?" I must have blocked her out for a minute. The salmon tasted amazing.

"Were you even listening to me? Online dating is what."

"Oh, that's not for me."

"How do you know? It's really fun. I've met a lot of interesting men that way."

"I'm sure you have," I said, rolling my eyes. I couldn't even imagine the types of guys Nancy was finding online. "Any keepers?"

"There's one that I like more than the rest."

"How many is the rest?"

"I don't know. I usually go on four or five dates a week."

I was more than a little shocked. I had been on two or three dates within the past few months. It just didn't seem right.

"Are you kidding me? How do you manage that?" I asked.

"I just do. Finding a husband is like a second job." Taking the last sip of her wine, she said, "You're the one who told me to start living life in this little, podunk town."

Silence.

"Close your mouth," she said. "It's so unbecoming."

I closed my mouth. The look of disbelief remained.

"Are all the men from around here?" I asked, perusing the restaurant patrons. I noticed more than a few sets of eyes gazing at the lovely Nancy. "Have you dated anyone sitting in this restaurant?" Most of them appeared to be with their wives, but then again maybe the whole place was filled with online daters.

"The men come from all over, even as far as the Cities. I've dated farmers, mechanics, lawyers, insurance salesmen, one optometrist, and even a hairstylist, who I swear was gay. I think he was still in denial. Anyway, meeting all these men is a lot more fun than sitting around watching television every night. You really should consider it. Just once. What do you have to lose?"

"My dignity."

"Geez, Kody. Where's your sense of adventure? Not to be mean or anything, but it wouldn't hurt for you to get out more. You remind me a lot of myself when I first moved to town."

That wasn't nice. So I was a little old-fashioned. I preferred a chance meeting with Mr. Right to a planned meeting with Mr. You-Looked-Better-Online. It would be my luck that the one time I did agree to go on a date with someone I met online he would be a serial rapist. He would wine and dine me, reel me in with his good looks and charm. Once we left the restaurant, I would get thrown into a rented minivan where he'd drive me to some remote location. With pure evil in his eyes, he'd rip away at my clothes and violate me in the worst ways imaginable. I'd be left bruised and battered on the side of the road unsure if anyone would stop to help before the hungry animals of the night smelled my blood and fear. Once again, my imagination took me to the dark side.

"I'll think about it," I said.

"We might even find a couple of men interested in a double date. Can you imagine?"

"Not really."

"I'll send you a link to the service I use so you can check it out. I think you'll be pleasantly surprised."

"Don't get your hopes up. I'll look at the site, but that's all I can promise."

"Good enough for me."

"Let's get back to Mary, shall we?" I said.

Together, we devised a plan aimed at building Mary's self-confidence. Even though Nancy had never met Mary, we made the assumption that if Mary looked good, she would feel good. That was part of the reason Nancy still dressed in designer clothes and heels. They made her feel good. As for me, a nice fitting pair of jeans and a t-shirt was all I needed. Hopefully we'd find Mary's happy place somewhere in between.

12

To: sad_dad1@gmail.com
From: kodyburkoff@inyourwords.com
Subject: I need more

Dear sad dad,

I was surprised to read in your last e-mail that you knew so much about me. Have we met before?

Your daughter's first few years of life sounded wonderful. She must have been a joy to be around. I couldn't help but notice though that this assignment didn't keep you entirely focused on her life. You still seem more focused on the boy's life. If you truly want help with your compulsion, you need to focus on the assignments I give you. I'm willing to help you, but I can't do that without your cooperation. When we're finished with your memoir, you don't want blank pages where warm sentiments should be, do you?

Your next assignment is to write about your favorite family vacations. Write about a trip to Mount Rushmore, a week at the lake, or what it was like the first time Julia saw and tasted the ocean. I want to hear about the car rides, plane rides, and walking tours. You can even include school field trips. Sometimes it's those short adventures that turn out to have the most influence. I know for me, I remember the many camping trips more than the one trip to Disney World.

As an added task, instead of sitting in your home typing your e-mail, why not grab a pencil and paper or a laptop and go somewhere that brings you good memories? Maybe you and Julia spent a lot of time at a particular park. Maybe you built her a tree house where she served you tea and mud pies. Don't rule out a road trip. Perhaps you have great memories from your days spent at the Mall of America. What kid doesn't have fun there? Do whatever you need to do to keep your focus on the good times you had with Julia. She deserves to be remembered that way.

Sincerely,
Kody

13

"I can't believe I let you talk me into this. Sam is a complete jerk," I said, stepping into Harry's Bar on Friday night.

"He's Jason's cousin. I have to be here. You, being my best friend, have a certain obligation."

"I have an obligation not to rat you out when you steal your kids' Halloween candy or when you lie to Jason about how much you spent on your hair. I do not have an obligation to attend parties thrown by egotistical maniacs."

"Wow! He really pissed you off."

"You could say that."

"He has a hard time talking to women. I remember feeling the same way when I first met him. Once you get past his macho exterior, he really is a sweet guy."

"He might be sweet if his mouth was …"

"Best manners," Kendall said, cutting me off. Sam had spotted us and was ducking around people to greet us. He could do that, you know. His only worry might be getting elbowed in the forehead.

"You look gorgeous, Kendall, as always." Looking at me with a smirk, he said, "I knew you couldn't stay away."

Kendall grabbed my hand as I turned to leave.

"I made her come," Kendall said. "Kody mentioned you made quite the impression the other day."

"My intentions weren't to offend you, Kody. I apologize if I did."

Who was this guy? Did he have to be accompanied by a family member to act like a civilized adult?

"Okay," I said, looking away.

Kendall excused us and we made a beeline for the bar. Knowing Kendall, her plan was to get me tipsy enough to want to stay.

With drinks in hand, Kendall and I mingled with the rest of the party-goers. We knew almost everyone so it was fun to see some people whom I hadn't seen in a while. When we first arrived, I thought I would have to spend the evening avoiding Sam, but he was too busy trying to build his customer base. Business before pleasure, I guess.

I spent a good portion of the night catching up with an old client of mine, Jimmy Nygard. Jimmy was a retired farmer who didn't normally like these sorts of events, but his wife, Esther, was running for mayor and insisted he come along for moral support. He sat alone at the bar sipping a whiskey sour. His wife worked the room in the same fashion as Sam.

Jimmy and I discussed the weather, of course, and then he went on to tell me about the latest dispute he was having with his neighbor, Earl. Jimmy and Earl hated each other. It wasn't always this way. At one time they were best friends. At one time they were also both in love with the same woman. Lucky for Jimmy, he won the prize and still held on to her.

Earl couldn't handle losing anything, especially the love of his life, Esther. Because of his anger, Earl tried to sabotage Jimmy's farm every chance he got, perhaps hoping that if Jimmy lost everything he might also lose Esther. Earl would go to Jimmy's late at night and open the gates around the property so that when Jimmy awoke in the morning his cows were wandering in the road. Earl also messed with Jimmy's rain gauge by filling it with water from the tap. When Jimmy was downtown at the café bragging, Earl called him a liar and a cheat in front of everyone. Those were fighting words no matter who you were.

While I listened to Jimmy tell yet another sordid tale, Kendall caught my attention. She didn't look happy. I excused myself and met her halfway.

"I could have used rescuing about ten minutes ago. Mrs. Owen had me cornered," Kendall said.

"Sorry about that," I said, not really meaning it.

"Did you know the older checkout woman at the supermarket is sleeping with one of the young bag boys? Talk about a cougar."

Kendall passing along the latest gossip learned from Mrs. Owen led me to believe that their conversation wasn't all that intolerable. My eyes wandered while she continued. I wasn't one for community gossip. I tried to keep my mind as clutter-free as possible. It wasn't always easy.

I locked eyes with the guest of honor. He scurried over as fast as those little legs allowed him to go. I know. Stop with the short jokes, right? I can't. It's just too much fun.

"Hey, gorgeous. Are you having a good time?"

"I was," I said, taking a step back.

Completely disregarding my body language and rude response, he said, "We should go out sometime, just you and me."

Kendall was quick to support his idea. "You totally should. We could be related some day."

I gave Kendall the look of death, which she easily ignored.

"You bet. We could give Kendall's kids some playmates," Sam said with raised eyebrows.

I wanted to puke.

"I'll pick you up tomorrow night at eight. Wear something sexy."

Before I could respond, Sam disappeared into the crowd of people.

"I cannot believe you just did that to me," I said, seething mad. "Am I the only one that sees him for what he is, a short, sexist pig?"

"He's a nice guy. Give him a chance. Plus, I know it's been weeks since you were on a date."

"I don't care if it's been *years*. I am not going out with him."

"Kody, you have to," Kendall said with pleading eyes.

"Tell me one good reason why."

"I'm sure I told you about this before, but Sam was engaged not too long ago and he's had a really hard time dealing with the loss."

Kendall made it sound as though Sam's fiancé died or something. I'm sure she just left his ass high and dry. She probably couldn't put up with his cocky attitude any longer.

"His fiancé was in a terrible car accident. She was in the hospital for about two months before she passed away. The accident happened only a few weeks before their wedding. Sam was crushed as you can imagine."

"Geez, Kendall. That still doesn't give him the right to treat women the way he does."

"I know it doesn't. I'll have Jason talk to him. He'll make sure he behaves himself."

I could not even believe I was feeling sorry enough for this guy to actually contemplate going out with him. I was an idiot, or worse, desperate.

"Please, Kody. It would mean a lot to Jason…and to me."

Again with the sad eyes. She was using all her tricks.

"Jason better work some serious magic," I said more than a little annoyed.

Kendall squealed with excitement while I envied the guests trickling out the door. I knew I was going to regret my decision the minute Sam opened his mouth. If not then, then for sure when we sat down at a restaurant and he started hitting on the waitress. That seemed like something he would do. I only hoped I could contain myself enough not to run screaming out the door.

14

To: kodyburkoff@inyourwords.com
From: sad_dad1@gmail.com
Subject: Family vacations

I'm sitting outside his house. He's watching television by himself. I don't think his parents or brother are at home. His car is the only one parked out in the street. This is the perfect time to kill him, when he least expects it. I'm sure Julia never expected to die when she did.

Looking at him in the comforts of his home makes me sick. My hands are clammy from squeezing the handle of my gun. I wouldn't be sitting here like this if the cops had got it right. If they had seen things my way, he would be sitting in jail right now trembling at the touch of another inmate.

Don't worry, Kody. He'll live another day. If I do decide to kill him, it won't be here. It'll be far away where no one will find him for days. I won't kill him right away either. He and I are going to have some words first. He's going to admit to murdering my little girl. He's going to admit to his wrongdoing.

I know this wasn't what you had in mind for my assignment. I was on my way to the park when I got distracted. Are you beginning to understand how strong my compulsion is?

sad dad

15

As promised, I was spending my Saturday with Anna so that Brian could take seven-year-old Ethan to a Twins game. I spotted them coming up the walkway, which forced me to clear my head of sad dad's latest words, "Don't worry, Kody. He'll live another day." Oh, okay. I won't worry then. I'll just forget everything that was written and not worry that a young man might die at the hands of an angry father. No problem.

The sight of Anna holding an adorable kitten pushed aside the nagging feeling I had that it was time to get the police involved. Brian never mentioned anything about cat-sitting too.

"I am so sorry about this. Anna was awfully persistent. I can take the cat back home if you want," Brian apologized.

"Don't worry about it. It's a nice surprise," I replied.

Brian had a hard time telling his kids no. His excuse was that he didn't want to see disappointment on their faces ever again since they lived through such disappointment when their mom was sick and eventually died. I didn't have the heart to tell him that at some point he was going to have to treat them like normal kids. This special treatment might actually hurt them more than help them. The three of them were still healing though, so my commentary would have to wait awhile longer.

I informed Anna of my list of ideas for us to do during our day together. The list included: painting our toenails, giving each other facials, making friendship bracelets, baking cookies, making silly putty, and watching *Enchanted*. I was all geared up to have a totally girly day. I even bought us matching pink bathrobes to lounge around in.

"That sounds like fun, Kody. Can we add something else too?" Anna asked.

"Sure, sweetie. What do you have in mind?"

Anna left the living room and marched off to the guest bedroom where she had tossed her backpack and pillow pet. She came back with what looked like a toilet seat.

"This is for Hermione, my kitten," she said, handing it to me.

I was reluctant to take the toilet seat not knowing where it might have been. I think anyone else would have done the same.

"It's clean. I haven't got to use it yet." Her expression was serious, yet hopeful.

"What are you planning to do with this?" I asked.

"Teach Hermione to go to the bathroom in it. I bought it online."

"You bought it online? Does your dad know about this?"

"He gave me his credit card. It's okay."

"He gave you his credit card? You're only ten. You shouldn't be ordering things online."

Oh, Brian. What are you doing to your children? Now it was harmless animal contraptions, but what about in a few years when Anna had other curiosities? He needed to wake up from the dream he was living in sooner than later.

"Okay, Anna," I sighed. She seemed completely unfazed by my lack of enthusiasm. Like her dad, I was not going to tell her no. "Explain to me how this cat toilet seat works and we'll see if Hermione is smart enough to use it."

Anna did as I asked with way more energy than I would have put forth being that the topic was cat excrement. We followed the instructions, all three of them, and were ready to put Hermione to the test. Unfortunately, the first test failed. The kitten immediately jumped down from the seat. Anna didn't get discouraged though because the instructions also clearly stated that this endeavor would take some time, but in the end be worth it. No more cleaning smelly cat boxes. No more buying bags of toxic cat litter. Oh, and get this, Anna can eventually order a motion-sensitive flusher for the cat to flush away her own deposits. Isn't that something?

Fortunately, Anna grew tired of chasing after Hermione to put her on the toilet seat. I only hoped the kitten was smart enough to find my cat's litter box, not that Percy was going to be thrilled with another cat's scent on her turf. I didn't want to step in a puddle of cat urine with my new pedicure.

The rest of the afternoon went as planned. We did all the girly things that were on my list. I even let Anna put makeup on me, which was a generous act being that I hated people touching my face. After a terrible bout with acne in my teens, I was paranoid about getting germs in my pores.

Brian knocked on my door while we were snuggled up watching *Enchanted* and eating the chocolate chip cookies we made earlier. Anna barely looked up when her dad walked in the room. I took it as a compliment that she was having a good time with me. Brian's expression told me that he had been ignored before and didn't appreciate it.

"Anna, let's get going, honey. Your brother is sleeping in the car."

"Can't I stay here with Kody?"

Knowing the question was coming, Brian said, "No, I'm sure Kody has plans tonight. Am I right?"

"Actually," I hesitated, "I do have a date tonight." Directing my next comment to Anna, I said, "We'll do this again. Okay?"

Anna nodded reluctantly. She was clearly disappointed, about as much as Brian was.

"A date, huh? With who, if you don't mind me asking?"

"You probably don't know him. He's Kendall's cousin. No, he's Jason's cousin. It doesn't really matter. I don't even want to go. I'm just doing it to appease Kendall. She basically begged me to go out with him."

Brian put his hands up motioning that I could stop talking at any time. "It's not a big deal, Kody. You're free to date whoever you want. You aren't hurting my feelings." He picked up Anna's bag and pillow pet. It was obvious from the shape of her bag that she remembered to pack Hermione's new toilet seat. "Have fun tonight and thank you for helping me out. I appreciate it."

"I'm glad I could help," I said.

Anna hugged me tight and they were off. I needed to get motoring as well. Sam and his sparkling personality would be arriving within the hour. Oh, how I dreaded tonight. Regardless, with all the pampering we did during the day, I was bound to go out looking good. There was always the chance I'd run into Mr. Right while out with Mr. Wrong.

* * * *

"Tell me about your day, gorgeous," Sam said, swirling the last bit of wine in his glass.

We were almost through drinking a glass of wine before he stopped talking about himself to ask me how my day was. I was already utterly annoyed and we hadn't even ordered our meal yet. His terms of endearment were out of control, as well as his wandering eyes. There wasn't a woman in the restaurant who had escaped his scrutiny.

Through gritted teeth, I said, "It was fine. I spent it with a ten-year-old if that tells you anything."

"I love kids. I hope to have a whole baseball team, which is why I look for a woman to have good birthing hips. It's important, you know," he said with a straight face. "I don't want a frail woman that can't push out a few centerfielders."

My jaw dropped. I had never heard anyone talk like that, much less talk to me like that. Screw Kendall. Some words needed to be said.

"I don't know who you think you are, but I am not going to put up with your rude behavior any longer. I don't have to sit here and take this verbal abuse. Kendall begged me to go out with you. She feels sorry for you. Did you know that? How is that for your oversized ego?"

I picked up my purse and left him sitting there looking as shocked as I had been only seconds before.

To hell with him. My birthing hips were no one's business.

It was still light out, the weather was perfect, and I needed to blow off some steam so I chose to walk the mile or so home instead of calling someone to pick me up. That someone wasn't going to be Kendall, mind you. She did not want to hear what I had to say right now.

As I strolled down the sidewalk, Sam's words played over and over again in my head. What a jerk. How did he plan on forming a baseball team when he treated women like livestock? And how the heck had the guy been engaged before? I didn't see anything positive that he had to offer.

Now, I, on the other hand, had a lot to offer. I was the total package. Any man, besides Sam, would be lucky to have me. I would find that one man eventually. The one to have children with. The one to grow old with. I was a big believer in fate and that was what was going to bring me together with my soul mate. I only wished fate worked quicker or had more defined deadlines. I really didn't want to find my soul mate while I was in menopause. For one, there went the prospect of having children. Second, I've heard those hot flashes were pretty intense. It would be nice to have a secure relationship before all that started happening. I couldn't be picky I guess. If I rushed fate, I might settle for someone I didn't truly love. What could be worse?

I turned the last corner before reaching my home. A car was sitting in the driveway. I didn't recognize it and because of the angle of the setting sun I was blinded from identifying the driver. Just like I did at my first funeral viewing, I clumsily flipped myself around and scampered behind a giant evergreen on the corner. I didn't want whoever was sitting in the car to see me if they hadn't already.

My first thought was of sad dad. I didn't even consider Sam coming over to apologize for his comments. He didn't see anything wrong with the way he spoke. Sam didn't scare me anyway. I knew how to handle him. I wasn't sure how to handle sad dad, however. What if he changed his mind and wanted to talk in person? What if he was angry because his compulsion to kill was still just as strong as before he began writing to me? What if he was planning to kidnap me and force me to witness him killing the boy? Ugh! There went my imagination again. But, seriously, all of those were valid questions. Oh, why didn't I call the police this morning?

The thought of contacting them had popped into my head numerous times throughout the day. I was struggling with what to tell them. I was also questioning if I had given my relationship with sad dad a fair chance. We had only written back and forth to each other a handful of times. Some of what he wrote was positive. Some of it wasn't. Was it too early to throw in the towel? Then again, was it too early to warn his victim? While staying hidden behind the evergreen waiting for my admirer to grow weary, I made a deal with myself. If I got inside and there was a redeeming message from sad dad, I'd give him another chance. If there was no message, I'd phone the police immediately. Not a popular decision, but a decision nonetheless.

After the car slowly backed out of my driveway and drove down the street in the opposite direction, I darted to my doorstep. The door hadn't been broken into, which was a good sign. No forced entry. Once inside, my paranoia took over and I checked every room. Nothing but dust bunnies and loose papers. Confident that my home was secure, I sat down to check my e-mail. With one eye open, I saw the direction I was being led. Sad dad had me for at least a little while longer.

16

To: kodyburkoff@inyourwords.com
From: sad_dad1@gmail.com
Subject: Family vacations

I want to apologize for my last e-mail. I wasn't in the right frame of mind earlier. I get like that sometimes. I sink so low that I justify to myself that murder is okay, which it isn't, because it wasn't okay for my daughter.

I'm at the park now sitting under the tree that Julia and I had our picnics under. She loved having picnics. When she was five and six years old we would come out here at least once a week in the summer. She even talked me into coming out here in the middle of the winter a few times. With all of our snow gear on we sipped hot chocolate and ate fruit snacks. It was something only her and I did, which made it very special. Gabe was just a toddler then so he wasn't allowed to join us. She liked having me all to herself. The feeling was mutual.

After we finished our picnic we played on the playground. She preferred the swings over the other equipment. I didn't mind at all pushing her for as long as she was entertained because while she swung she told me stories. Some stories were about kids in preschool and kindergarten. Others were about Gabe. Even when she grew older she felt comfortable telling me stories about her classmates, which is why I was surprised that I hadn't heard about the new kid in town. She never mentioned him. Being that I was at the elementary school, I didn't know about the new family. Their kids were both older.

It's hard being here at this park. I can see her. I can see her smile with those little gaps that her baby teeth left behind. Her long straight hair was always hanging loose on her neck even on the hottest days. She hated wearing her hair up. When her mom convinced her to wear a ponytail or braids, there were still wisps blowing into her eyes.

That reminds me of the time our family took a trip to Colorado. Julia was eleven and Gabe was eight. We were on a very tame whitewater rafting adventure on the Arkansas River. Once again Julia refused to wear her hair back. She was really into her looks then and spent a lot of time in front of a mirror. Well, the wind began to pick up, as did the rapids, and Julia's hair got into her eyes. I witnessed the look of pure irritation, not unfamiliar to me and her mother, right before she threw down her oar. With her hands free, she angrily piled every loose strand of hair on her head and held it there with both hands for the rest of the raft ride. We all have our breaking point and that was apparently Julia's. Gina and I were furious with her at the time because she refused to contribute to the adventure we had all been waiting months for. Later that night, however, after Julia and Gabe were in bed and we had some alone time on the balcony of our hotel room, we shared a good laugh arguing over which one of us Julia took after. The image of our daughter and how ridiculous she looked on that raft brought tears to Gina's eyes, tears of laughter, that is.

We had some good times back then. Life was so simple. It was truly the little things that made us laugh. I remember the time Julia begged and begged us to let her have her first sleepover. We caved, of course. She was only eight at the time and was determined to have her best friend of the week, Kennedy, spend the night. Gina called Kennedy's parents to get all the details worked out. Kennedy arrived at dinner time to eat pizza with us. Julia insisted on one kind of pizza claiming that it was the kind you had at sleepovers. The rest of the night went along rather smoothly, or so we thought. The girls had locked themselves in Julia's room to do whatever it was eight-year-old girls did. I didn't really want to know to tell you the truth.

While Gina and I sat on the couch watching television, trying to relax, Julia burst into the room in tears. She refused to tell us what was wrong. A few seconds later, Kennedy walked into the room. From the looks of her, it was evident that the girls had got into some makeup. Kennedy's eyes were completely blacked out. She looked like a raccoon. As it turned out, the girls were playing "puppies" and wanted to make each other look like one. Julia couldn't find any suitable product in the collection of old makeup Gina had given her so they decided to use a black Sharpie to create the look of a Dalmatian. I was barely able to keep my composure. Gina didn't think it was very funny at the time so my smirk was met with "that look" she was so famous for. I knew she was pondering how she was going to explain this to Kennedy's parents in the morning.

Not wanting the marker to soak into the poor child's skin more than it already had, Gina took to scrubbing Kennedy's eyes until they were red with still a hint of gray. She then sent the girls to bed saying that they should try again in the morning. It wasn't until later that night that Gina found humor in the matter. She leaned over from her side of the bed and pulled a Sharpie from behind her back. With uncontrollable laughter, I fought that crazy woman off me. Her playfulness was appreciated, but part of me really thought she might mark up my face. I didn't know how I would explain that to my students on Monday morning.

I have so many great memories, ones with all of us happy, enjoying each other's company. I'll never get those moments back. I guess no one ever does. Kids grow up, adults change. The past remains the past. We all must move on, look forward.

I feel better now. Maybe this will work after all. It was a lot of fun remembering Colorado and the infamous makeup mess-up. What's next? I feel like I'm on a roll.

sad dad

17

"I've never gone out with a bigger jerk," I said to Kendall. She reluctantly agreed to meet me Sunday morning for bagels and coffee. I planned to let her know just how awful the previous night's date was. She knew what was coming.

"Jason talked to him, told him to take his personality down a notch," was all she said. I was hoping for a little more than that. She was merely passing the buck.

"Do you know what it feels like to have someone look at you and have the guts to comment on your birthing hips? It's disgusting. My hips are my business. He had no right to say that to me. Nor did he have the right to call me every sickening pet name he could think of. He makes all men look bad. I think I'm scarred for life from what happened last night."

Kendall rolled her eyes. "More scars, Kody?"

Now I was really fired up.

"Where's the compassion, Kendall?" I said, dropping my bagel on the plate.

"I'm sorry. I'm sorry you had such a terrible time last night. I wouldn't have asked..."

"Begged."

"Fine. I wouldn't have begged you to go out with him if I thought he would behave so poorly. I've never seen that side of him."

"I don't get that. He must have some sort of split personality or something."

"Maybe. Jason's family has some suspicious characters." Kendall took a sip of her coffee. "If it makes you feel any better, while you were out having a horrible time with Sam, I was at home dealing with a three-year-old from hell."

"No, it doesn't make me feel any better."

Ignoring my remark, she continued. "He is so damn sneaky and does whatever he wants. It's like he doesn't care what we say. Our words mean nothing to him."

I didn't want to change the subject, but her description reminded me of someone.

"He sounds a lot like sad dad," I said under my breath.

"You're still communicating with him?" Kendall asked with a disgusted look on her face.

"Yes," I sighed. "I'm still trying to fix another broken soul."

"Do you feel like you're doing any good? Is he getting better?"

"I'm not sure. I think it's too early to tell." I bit off another piece of my blueberry bagel. "Do you think sad dad is someone we know?"

Kendall's eyes grew big. Uh-oh. I probably shouldn't have said that.

"Why? What happened?"

"Ah, nothing," I said, not making eye contact.

"Something happened. What aren't you telling me?"

I really didn't want to tell her. She was going to go nuts if she found out sad dad knew we were friends and that he made a comment about her children. Maybe I should make up something. She would see right through it. She saw through my lie about having my teeth whitened. For whatever reason, I chose to lie to Kendall about this. I denied it for weeks. Some people lied about a nose job or about getting breast implants. I chose teeth whitening. She didn't let it go until I finally gave in and confessed the truth. I couldn't

85

handle the guilt any longer. After I told her, she acted as if she had just won a marathon. I, on the other hand, felt like a complete loser even with my strikingly white smile.

"Sad dad might have mentioned you in an e-mail," I said, wincing in preparation for her reaction.

"Are you kidding me? What did he say? Why didn't you tell me? What if he's been stalking us for weeks, or maybe even months?"

"Relax."

"Don't tell me to relax. After what happened with you and Daniel, I have every right to get upset when you tell me about another one of your crazy clients. I can't believe this is happening again!"

"Nothing is happening again. He hasn't directed anything threatening toward you or me. He's still focused on the boy that killed his daughter. He's trying to turn it around. His last e-mail was much better. There was hardly a reference to death or murder. I really don't think we have anything to worry about."

Kendall leaned back in her chair. "You know what it is? Facebook. You think everyone wants to be your friend so you accept requests from anyone with an account."

Hmm. She had a point. I did have a bad habit of accepting friend requests when I didn't know the people. I didn't know she knew that. I thought it was my little secret.

"You must have over a thousand friends," Kendall said, using finger quotes around the word friends.

She was visibly upset. I couldn't blame her. Daniel had changed us both. I installed alarms on my office doors and Kendall did a background check on anyone she didn't know. Fear made people do crazy things.

While I pulled up Facebook on my phone, Kendall went off about how irresponsible I was, about how my choices not only affected me but the people surrounding me. She then pulled Jason into the mix because apparently he was irresponsible too. Poor guy. He wasn't even here to defend himself and he was getting a lecture. That was marriage for you.

Kendall and Jason were another couple that didn't experience love right away. They met in college and hung out with the same crowd on the weekends. After knowing each other for almost a year, Jason finally asked her out. She said he wasn't the cutest or smartest guy she had ever met, but he was funny. They ended up dating for four years, got married, and now have two adorable little boys and seemed to be relatively happy.

It's not the most exciting love story I've ever heard. Of course, Kendall also thinks that's why I'm so miserable at finding love. She thinks I've already written my love story in my head and am now looking to cast the part for the leading male role. I have to admit I know how I want my story to read, or not to read. I've dated enough men, talked to enough people, and read enough books to know that my story has a slim chance, which is enough of a chance for me.

"One thousand fifty-nine," I read from my Facebook page.

"Are you kidding me? You don't have that many friends."

"Gee, thanks. I can't help it that I'm more popular than you," I said with a smirk. "He's probably one of them, I guess. How am I ever going to find him in this mess?"

"You'll just have to go through them one by one," Kendall said.

"That will take forever, and then what if we're wrong? What if he's not a friend? Do I ask him what kind of car he drives?"

Dang it. I did it again. Was I subconsciously looking to get ridiculed by my best friend? Every time I opened my mouth I was giving Kendall one more tidbit of information to set her off. My intentions for meeting her for coffee were so that I could give her a hard time for setting me up with Sam. I was supposed to be the one with the angry face.

"There's something else you aren't telling me, isn't there Kody? You better speak up. We don't need any more secrets."

"Are you going to ground me if I don't tell you?" I said sarcastically. Sometimes Kendall fell into "mommy mode" and spoke to me like I was her child. I had to give her credit. She was definitely scarier than my mom ever was.

"No, but we're going to the cabin soon and I want to make sure I have time to rescue you before I leave."

"I won't need rescuing," I whined. "Not every client is going to turn out like Daniel."

"You don't know that. This guy might be worse."

"Or he might be completely harmless."

Kendall was too annoyed to speak. She was probably thinking about what an idiot I was for fantasizing that sad dad was harmless. Was I an idiot? I had to wonder given that sad dad's first e-mail to me included the subject line, "Stop my compulsion to kill," and in one of his last messages he was sitting outside his potential victim's house contemplating murder. Hmm.

"When I walked home from my date with Sam there was a car parked in my driveway," I admitted.

Kendall perked up and her expression quickly changed from annoyance to intrigue.

"I don't know who it was and I didn't recognize the car," I continued." The angle of the sun made it really hard to see. Whoever it was wasn't trying to hide. For that reason, I'm not so sure it was sad dad."

With my confession, Kendall completely dropped the attitude and we spent the next several minutes discussing absolutely every angle of sad dad and his compulsion. I knew Kendall was really trying to ease my nerves. She knew me better than anyone. She knew I tried to mask my fears, especially when I was working with someone like sad dad.

Was it possible that I was the only one that knew of sad dad's compulsion to kill? He mentioned that his family and friends were made uncomfortable by his anger and most likely his obsession with finding justice for his daughter. They had to have some idea. But did anyone else know how close he was to acting on his compulsion?

18

To: sad_dad1@gmail.com
From: kodyburkoff@inyourwords.com
Subject: I'm proud of you

Dear sad dad,

The stories you shared in your last e-mail were great. I especially liked the Sharpie story. I can imagine what that must have looked like. It's amazing what kids will do! Let's keep things moving along since you feel like we're making progress.

Let's add even more stories from Julia's childhood. Tell me who she dressed up as for Halloween. Tell me about the first time she rode a bike or about the first fish she caught. Tell me about her hidden talents. Did she draw or tell funny jokes? Could she wiggle her ears or move her eyebrows? Did she have to dance everywhere she went? Did she have a favorite song or movie that she played over and over again?

It might help if you looked at her baby books or at old videos you might have stored on your computer. These will help jog your memory. They, of course, might also draw out other emotions.

Don't let the anger and sadness take over. Keep focused on the happiness and excitement you felt when you watched Julia do something for the first time. Surely the positive thoughts outweigh the negative.

About Gabe, like you said, kids grow up and adults change. Your relationship with your son is likely to change too. You have to realize that your son lost his sister. He is struggling with the loss just as you are. Keep trying to talk to him. Break that barrier that's been building since Julia's death, or from even before. I'm sure Julia would have wanted the two of you to continue being a family.

You can do this! I'm very proud of you!

Kody

19

I parked in the back alley as usual. The only thing I did differently on this start to the work week was make sure the coast was clear before leaving my car to enter my office. I knew Sam was probably next door getting his office space together and I did not want to lay eyes on that man, especially when I was suffering from PMS and the guilt of involving Kendall in my work mess yet again. My mood wasn't helped when I spotted Charlie approaching my door before I had a chance to get settled. The roller coaster hadn't even loaded yet and he appeared to be down in the dumps. Obviously, he didn't get lucky last night.

"Good morning, Kody," he murmured upon entering. With his head hung, shoulders slumped, and a blank look on his face, he stopped near the front table where we sat the other day.

PMS or not, I forced myself to get happy. I wasn't about to climb aboard the Mood Swing Enterprise. Too many loop-the-loops for me. In my peppiest tone, I responded, "Hey, Charlie. Another sunny day, huh?"

"Sure is," he said before wandering to the back of the office where it was dark. He plopped himself down into the leather recliner.

"I'm not on top of my game today. My ex called me over the weekend."

My quizzical expression led him to announce which ex he was talking about.

"Catherine. She's getting out of jail tomorrow and wanted to know if she could stay with me for a while, until she gets a job lined up and finds a place to live."

"Oh. That's short notice. What did you tell her?"

"I told her yes. I didn't know what else to say. I was completely taken aback by her call. We haven't spoken since the night before she left me."

"Do you think she's hoping to get back together with you?"

"Oh, I don't know. I don't know what she's thinking. I can't just let her waltz into my life again though. It was her choice to leave, even after all the hours of counseling I endured and everything I had to do to convince my friends that she wasn't going to steal their shit anymore. I deserved more than a note taped to the coffee pot."

"You certainly did."

Charlie leaned forward in the recliner and rested his head in his hands. "I'm ashamed to say it, but I still love her. I can't change the way I feel."

Love was funny that way. It didn't always allow you to make sensible decisions, and more often than not, it caused a lot of heartache and frustration.

"Of course, you do. You wouldn't have married her if you didn't," I said, trying to console his aching heart.

"Well, what about the woman I'm seeing now, the one I told you about the other morning? She's not going to stick around if my ex-wife comes traipsing back into my life. I might not be in love with her, but we sure as hell have a lot of fun together."

"That's a tricky situation. You need to be very honest with this new woman and Catherine. It will be interesting to say the least." Wanting to lighten up the situation, I said, "Maybe you'll be the prize possession of both women. They just might agree to share you."

That got his wheels spinning. Simply imply something somewhat sexual to get a man's imagination rolling.

"Now that would be something, wouldn't it? Having two women share the rights to old Charlie Reynolds."

It was nice to see a smile on his face even if it was inspired by naughtiness.

"I'm sure it's easier said than done," I said.

"You got that right, but it would be fun to give it a try. I've always wanted to…"

"Don't finish that statement," I interrupted, plugging my ears.

"What? I was only going to say…"

"Charlie, we should really get to work on your memoir." I was serious. I had no interest in learning about his fantasy with two women. My imagination was also rolling and the visuals were already starting to invade my skull.

"We really don't have that much left anyway. We've already documented everything from your childhood to the end of your second marriage. From the sounds of it though, you'll have a whole lot to include in the very near future. Do you want me to hang on to this when we're done or are you in a hurry to get a printed copy in your hands?"

He thought about it for a while, which made me question his desire to write a memoir in the first place. He was a young enough guy who still had a lot of life to live, and from what I knew he wasn't suffering from an incurable disease. I was under the impression that Charlie simply wanted to tell his story for himself. His parents were both dead and he never had any children so it wasn't like he had anyone close to leave it with.

"Can I get back to you on that?" he asked, looking rather serious.

"Of course."

Charlie and I spent the next half hour discussing his hit and miss relationships after his second wife divorced him. He also went into great detail about his job working at the grain mill. I had never really understood how all that worked so I was actually enlightened by our conversation.

When his time was up, he looked to be in a much better mood than when he arrived. He departed promising to keep me up to date on his love life. I wished him the best of luck.

The rest of the morning went along without any surprises. I heard construction noises next door, but I had yet to lay eyes on the little man running the show. If he was smart, he would give me a few more days to calm down before barging in to apologize, if that was even his plan. Honestly, he probably had no idea why I left the restaurant. Short and stupid.

Giving my eyes a much needed break from the screen, I watched as a few people passed by my front windows. They were mostly construction workers, with a few others on their way to the bank or the hardware store on the corner. One man immediately caught my eye. He was a good-looking guy dressed in shorts, a t-shirt, a hat, and Teva sandals. His not wearing a cheap pair of flip-flops said a lot about him. My curiosity was piqued. He appeared to be either looking for someone or some place. I thought about going out to ask if he needed help, but I didn't want to risk seeing Sam. Terrible of me, I know. It wasn't until he took off his hat and sunglasses and cupped his hands around his eyes to peer through my window that I knew who he was. I knew that face.

I knew more than his face. I knew his soul. The man peering through my window had once made me the happiest girl in the world. He had once been my biggest fan, encouraging me to follow my dreams wherever they might lead. He knew all my fears, my joys, my passions. He taught me to love myself for who I was and not who I wanted to be. At one time, he was my prince charming.

My heart raced, but my excitement quickly turned to sadness, then fear, then to a sort of nervousness that I hadn't felt in ages as my mind flashed back to the summer after we both graduated from high school—the best and worst summer of my life. Was he here to talk about what happened? Or was he here just to say hello?

He didn't proceed to open the door. Instead, he remained outside shuffling his feet as though he was second-guessing his decision to visit me after all these years. I didn't know what to do so I sat as still as possible hoping that he might chicken out and leave the past alone. Whether I was ready to see him again or not, he finally pulled the door open and stepped inside.

He didn't say anything at first. Neither did I. Our eyes did all the talking. I felt an immediate connection. My body tingled all over just like the first time we kissed and meant it. Regardless of the event that put the lights out on our relationship, I felt a small spark for the boy in the man's body.

"Hello, Kody," he said.

"Paul," I said, still staring. "Long time, no see."

Our trance was broken by the ringing of his cell phone. While he fidgeted with the phone to presumably reject the call, I began fiddling with papers on my desk to give the impression that I had loads of work to do. If he had got any closer he would have seen that my "work" papers were really printouts of lake cabins to rent by the week.

"That was my dad. He calls me all the time now that I live back at home."

I nodded. More awkward silence.

"I saw your mom at the supermarket the other day. She told me about your new business. Congratulations."

"Thank you. She mentioned you were back in town. Divorced, huh?"

Way to go, Kody. Start talking about his failed marriage. That was bound to lead somewhere positive.

"She told you." Paul checked his watch and then put his hands in his pockets. "Yeah, my marriage didn't last too long. I could only handle three years with her. She was a real piece of work."

"I'm sorry to hear that," I said, still sitting at my desk. I didn't know if I should invite him to sit down or not. I didn't know the purpose for his visit.

"I…um…I've been thinking about you a lot lately, since I moved back to Wilcox, that is. It's hard not to think about the past when some of our old classmates are still living there. Did you know Johnny Milton owns the car dealership outside of town?" He crept a few steps closer. "Of course, you did. That shocked me though. I figured him as a roadie or something to do with heavy metal bands."

"My parents bought their last car from him. He's a different person from in high school," I said.

Looking down at his feet, he replied, "I bet that's the case for most people. I'm sure I'll learn that over time."

"I'm sure you will. How long do you plan on staying?"

"I don't know. A few years, I guess. My dad wants to semi-retire so he and my mom can start travelling. He wants me to run the store while he's away. With the divorce, it seemed like a good opportunity. I'm all about starting over."

Starting over, huh? Did he have aspirations of starting over with me? I shuffled more papers.

"Well, I can see that you're busy. I was in town so I figured I'd stop in to say hi. Walking toward the door to let himself out, he slowed and then turned around. "I also came to say I'm sorry, Kody. I'm truly sorry about what happened that summer."

Paul stood with the door open waiting for me to say something. I couldn't. I didn't. I let him walk away just as I did that day so many summers ago.

* * * *

The summer after high school graduation, I did what other normal teenagers did. I went to parties until all hours of the night. I spent time at friends' lake cabins getting the best tan possible. I also spent every waking moment with Paul before he and I went off to college. We were inseparable. The only time we were apart was when we were at work or when our friends demanded our undivided attention. Some might even say we were in love.

Even though Paul planned to attend college on the east coast while I was staying close to home, we intended to stay together. We thought that what we had could withstand the distance. Our friends told us we were crazy. They all thought we should break up to enjoy all that college had to offer, including the freedom to hook up with random guys and girls at parties. Neither of us was interested though. We never said it out loud, but neither of us intended for our relationship to ever be over.

That's why I never would have guessed what happened next.

Something went missing: my period.

I made the realization one morning when I was getting ready to go to work at the supermarket. I spied my feminine hygiene products pushed back behind the hair dryer that I stopped using once school got out and couldn't remember when I had used them last. Was it in May before the graduation ceremony? Did I have my period in June? Feeling the panic start to rise, I looked in the mirror at my larger, tender breasts. I convinced myself they were finally deciding to bust out of their A-cup to join the real world. And how about my mood swings lately? I was usually a pretty even-keeled person, but I was being a real bitch to Paul. Some of the things I said were unexplainable.

I immediately called Paul to tell him what I feared. He asked me if I was sure. I told him no and that he needed to buy a pregnancy test. The angry me told him it was the least he could do. He didn't argue.

Once I had the test in hand, I made him leave. He had hesitated in his offer to stay and honestly the sight of him only made me angrier. Even without learning the results of the test, I blamed him for not being better about using protection. He promised me nothing bad would happen. I believed him.

After he left, I sat on the bathroom floor crying my eyes out. No one was home so I could be as loud as I needed to be. I was scared. This wasn't how I had pictured my life. Being a pregnant teenager had never entered my mind. There was an order in which things happened and having a baby before a husband and career wasn't right. My dreams of living and working in New York City didn't include anyone but Paul. This wasn't supposed to happen to me.

Squatting over the toilet, I held the stick between my legs and urinated as instructed. The result was immediate. I called Paul and demanded that he buy another test, this time a different brand. I needed confirmation and I wasn't about to take the word of just one test. All the commercials said they were 99.9 percent accurate. I hoped to be in that .1 percent. No such luck. The second stick showed positive as well.

It was at that moment that I realized a living being was growing inside of me. A living being that relied on me to survive. I freaked out and screamed as loud and as long as I could until my throat burned and made me stop. I didn't want anything inside of me. I wasn't ready to be responsible for anyone but myself. This wasn't supposed to happen to me.

I called Paul to tell him the results of the second test. Since he'd had a few hours for the news to soak in, I was expecting him to try to calm me down and tell me everything was going to be okay. I was expecting him to say that he'd stand by me the entire way, that this wasn't anything we couldn't handle together. That's not what I heard. He instead asked me what I was going to do about it. Me. What was *I* going to do about it? Was this the same Paul that so lovingly convinced me our relationship could withstand the distance when he left for college?

Not knowing what else to say, I told him I would figure it out and hung up.

He called a few times, but I never answered the phone. When he came to the house, I told my parents to send him away. My parents asked a lot of questions because of my sudden change in behavior. I told them Paul cheated on me. They didn't ask any more questions only because they didn't want to believe that my friends and I were sexually active.

After days of dwelling over my situation, I came up with a plan on my own. It was a plan that made logical sense to me, yet it tore at my heart. I was going to have an abortion. Paul, happy that I had finally agreed to speak to him, didn't try to talk me out of it. Even if he had tried, I was ready to tell him that it was my body and he had no say over my decision. Paul called the closest abortion clinic and set up the appointment.

It was never the same between us. Paul kept his distance and I let him. I was so hurt by his reaction to the news of my being pregnant that it was hard to even look at him. I felt like I had been tricked into believing that he was someone worthy of my love. If he was scared, he could have told me. I made it very clear how I felt. I didn't understand why he was choosing to bottle up his emotions. We used to tell each other everything. Didn't we?

While waiting for the appointment date, I kept busy by focusing on my future as a college freshman. I purchased some last minute items for my dorm room, said good-bye to the friends I had been ignoring the past several weeks, and boxed up most of my personal items so that when my mom transformed part of my room into her craft area our things didn't get mixed up. I forgot about being pregnant for those few weeks. I almost felt normal.

Two nights before I was scheduled to be rid of the growing fetus inside of me, I woke up writhing in pain. To describe the pain as severe menstrual cramps was an understatement. I had never felt anything like it. My hands moved down my body wanting to rub away the hurt. They stopped when they felt the dampness of my pajama bottoms. I turned on my lamp for further inspection. I wished I hadn't because under those covers it looked like someone had been murdered. It only took a second for me to realize what had happened. I was again without child.

Ignoring the pain, I raced to the bathroom to clean up the mess as quietly as possible. While rinsing the washcloth, I paused to peer at my reflection in the mirror. The woman (I could no longer call myself a girl) before me was different somehow. The woman peering back at me had just lost a child that she had no intention of keeping. That same woman also felt tremendous guilt for having created it in the first place.

I never told anyone about the miscarriage except Paul. I figured he deserved to know what happened to our baby. As I bawled through my account of the previous night, he sat silent, his hands folded in his lap. Not once did he reach for me. Not once did he say, "It's going to be okay, Kody." He didn't even ask me how I was feeling. When I was done ranting about what a horrible mother I would have been anyway, I told him to leave. I told him I never wanted to see him again.

* * * *

He did as I asked until today.

20

To: kodyburkoff@inyourwords.com
From: sad_dad1@gmail.com
Subject: I'm proud of me too

The last few days have felt really good. I'm staying positive. The days are long and beautiful. I even invited a friend to play golf this weekend and he accepted. I feel like the old me has returned. I just hope it lasts. I'm scared something will trigger those negative thoughts again. It will always be a fear of mine. It's up to me to channel that fear into something else, like playing golf with a buddy.

Like most girls, Julia wanted to be a Disney princess for Halloween. This lasted for about five years. She was Snow White, Arial, Cinderella, Pocahontas, and I think Sleeping Beauty. We had all the dresses, shoes, and tiaras you could imagine. Until probably second grade, she dressed up in those costumes all the time. When our son was old enough, he joined her in the costume frenzy. It was fun seeing them play together even if it meant watching my only son wear glass slippers.

Our house (Gina's house now) is located near a retention pond. Surprisingly, the city keeps it stocked with mostly sunfish and bass, big and small mouth. The first few weeks after Gabe was born, I took Julia fishing there quite often. It got her out of the house and gave her my undivided attention. She used her pink princess pole and reeled in fish after fish. I barely had time to cast my own line in the water. After the first fish she caught I asked her if she wanted to kiss it good-bye. She did. Thereafter, she kissed every last fish she caught. When I told Gina about Julia's act of kindness, she cringed, which made Julia want to do it even more. It was years before she stopped kissing those fish good-bye.

Julia could do the splits at an early age. Granted, Gina had her enrolled in gymnastics classes when she was only two years old. She was also able to touch her nose with her tongue and count to one hundred at the age of four. She sounds like an amazing girl, huh?

Julia, of course, loved to watch all the Disney movies when she was younger. I would say her favorite fairy tale was Cinderella. The idea of having a fairy godmother appealed to her. Who didn't want someone to make all their dreams come true? As she grew older, she liked watching those twins' movies. I can't remember their names. I heard they were millionaires now. In high school she enjoyed all types of movies. Her and her friends were always at the theater. I can't even begin to tell you what her favorite one was.

You're right. Julia would have wanted Gabe and me to become close, to build a lasting relationship. She knew we had more differences than similarities. It's not easy though when he only comes to my place twice a week and then barely acknowledges my existence. He's here physically, but mentally, I don't know where that kid is. He's so much more complicated than I ever was, that's for sure. I wish we could have a normal relationship. I can't tell if he's scared of me or outright hates me. He holes himself up in his room before and after dinner. The only time I force him out of his room is to eat with me. Gina tells me to leave him alone. She says he's healing in a different way. I guess I should be thankful that he's not taking after his old man. The last thing this world needs is a teenager with an itch to kill.

Besides that last comment, I feel good about what I just wrote. For the most part, it's another good day.

sad dad

21

To: sad_dad1@gmail.com
From: kodyburkoff@inyourwords.com
Subject: Let's keep going

Isn't it amazing how all little girls love dressing up like princesses? I used to do the same thing when I was Julia's age. My favorite fairy tale was Cinderella too. I loved how she won the prince over and her evil stepmother and stepsisters got what they deserved.

Julia's obituary mentioned that she was "adventurous and was willing to try anything." Let's have your next e-mail focus on those details. I'd also love to hear who she got this trait from, you or your wife. Or maybe she came up with it on her own. Not every part of our personality can be traced to someone in the family.

Kody

22

Got what they deserved? I reread the e-mail message I sent to sad dad, regretting how I phrased my summation of Cinderella. Did I have to say it like that? I should have said Cinderella forgave her evil stepmother and stepsisters promising to never retaliate against them later in life. It sounded right being that Cinderella was so nice, but who knows how nice she was when she grew older. I know that when I was younger I let certain behaviors slide. Now, not so much. Let's take Sam for example. If I had dated Sam in college, I probably would have simply ignored him until he left me alone. I didn't have the guts back then to tell him what a horrible person he was. So, all I'm saying is that we don't know what type of person Cinderella develops into when she reaches thirty or forty. Can you imagine watching a movie about a middle-aged woman singing to the animals?

I heard whistling. The seven dwarves? Good grief, Kody. Get your head out of Walt Disney's ass and join the real world.

Walking up front to get a closer look at what was going on outside, I saw what could have been a soft drink commercial. Nancy was strolling up the sidewalk, assumingly headed in my direction, while an audience of construction workers from next door ogled her every step. Now that she was in my sights, I was hypnotized too. The warm, gentle breeze wafted her chestnut hair off her slender shoulders that were barely covered by the thin spaghetti straps of her silky aqua-blue dress. Her long, tanned legs led to a pair of spindly high heels showing the muscle tone in her calves with every step. She was an absolute vision of beauty, a real head-turner, and she had the full attention of every male, and female for that matter, in the vicinity. Damn her!

"Hi, Kody," Nancy said as I held the door open for her.

"You enjoyed that, didn't you?" I asked.

"Very much so."

We broke into laughter so evil only a woman could relate. We clearly understood the sheer magnetism women held over the opposite sex. We, however, could never understand the instinct and overwhelming drive of the male psyche. There was no doubt in our minds that there was only one thing on those men's minds as they drooled over Nancy when she walked past. It was truly amazing what a man would do for a piece of ass. It didn't always have to be a good piece of ass either.

"Mary's not here yet?" Nancy asked.

"She should be here any minute. Now remember, when I introduce the two of you she's going to be extremely shy. She has zero self-confidence and with you looking the way you do, she'll be even more introverted."

"What? I love this dress," Nancy said, peering down at herself.

"And you look lovely wearing it. I should have told you to tone it down a bit this first day, although, maybe you'll inspire her."

"Me inspire someone? That makes me nervous. I've never been anyone's role model before."

"You'll do great. Speaking of doing great, how's your date-athon going? Meet anyone over the weekend that will end this ridiculous love escapade?"

"I had dates Friday and Saturday night. Friday night was with a mechanic from town. Saturday was with a nutritionist from St. Paul.

They were both really nice, but neither of them really did it for me. I'll just have to keep looking," she said with a smile.

"Doesn't it get old not finding the right one?"

"I don't know. You tell me. Doesn't it get old not finding the right one?" she asked.

"We're talking about you right now."

"We might as well be talking about you."

"If you really want to know, I was on a date Saturday night too. It might have been the worst date I've ever been on. That's the honest truth." I motioned for Nancy to have a seat. Her towering over me in those heels made me uncomfortable. "You can't tell me out of all the dates you've been on lately there hasn't been one that was absolutely miserable."

Nancy thought for a moment and then hesitated. She was holding something back.

"You can tell me. I know you must have met at least one doofus in your search."

"I don't want to scare you away from online dating."

"You can't scare me away. I have no desire to date crazies found on the Internet, so spill it. What happened?"

"Well, there was this one guy. He spent the entire date trying to impress me with who he knew, who his clients were, and then he called me, "Honey," "Sugar," "Darling," and even "Hot Stuff" during dinner. I thought the date would never end."

Annoying pet names? Could it be?

"Was he really short?" I asked.

"Yeah, he only came up to my shoulders. When we were standing I felt like he was staring at my boobs. Actually, I felt like he was staring at my boobs while we were sitting down too. Why do you ask?"

"Was his name Sam? Sam Snyder?"

"How did you…oh, that was who you went out with on Saturday night?"

I nodded.

"Oh my gosh, Kody! What are the odds?"

"Fairly high, actually. There aren't a plethora of eligible, single men in town. You should know that by now. You've probably dated most of them."

"I am expanding the boundaries."

"Of course you are. The pickings are slim." I wanted to continue bagging on Sam so I said, "Wasn't he the biggest jerk you've ever met?"

"Not quite. I lived in Las Vegas, remember?"

"I still can't get that night out of my head," I said, noticing Mary parking her car across the street. "Mary's here. We can talk more about this later, if we even want to waste our breath on someone like Sam. Do you mind having a seat in the back and we'll join you in a second. I want to make sure Mary is feeling up to this before we get started."

"Sure thing."

My plan was set in motion. Mary sauntered across the street with no pep in her stride.

"Mary, how are you?" I asked, holding the door for her.

"I'm fine, thank you," she replied.

It was obvious she was lying.

"You're not fine. Which one of the sparkling personalities in your home made your morning not so bright?"

"Well, I'll let you choose. It could be my husband who left the house this morning still refusing to explain why he came home late last night, or it could be my stepdaughter who threw a fit because her black, sequined tank top was still in the dirty clothes hamper. I told her she was more than capable of washing her own clothes, for which she replied, 'That's your job. Why else are you home all day?'"

"Oh. Tough choice. But you know what? I'm not going to choose because I have a surprise for you."

"A surprise?"

"Do you remember my friend Nancy I mentioned to you last week?"

Mary nodded.

"Nancy is sitting in the back waiting to meet you. She's going to help with your makeover."

"Makeover? You never mentioned a makeover."

True. I had kept this a secret from Mary only because I figured she would say she didn't deserve it or she had no one to look pretty for.

"It's going to be fun. Trust me," I said, pulling her by the arm to the back where Nancy was sitting comfortably reading a magazine.

I introduced the two women. Mary's eyes widened at the sight of Nancy. I knew exactly what she was thinking, "I'll never look like her." To keep her from turning around and leaving I took her hand and sat her on the loveseat next to me. This was when I told Mary my plan to transform her into a woman proud to look in the mirror, maybe even proud enough to step on stage again.

Mary listened intently, swiveling her head from side to side as both Nancy and I elaborated on the details of her upcoming day. While we debated about where to meet for lunch, Mary yelled out, "Wait, wait, wait!" We immediately shut our mouths.

"Why?" Mary asked. "Why are you doing this?"

"What do you mean? Doesn't it sound like fun?" I replied.

"Yes, of course. What the two of you have planned sounds marvelous. But why? Why do you want to help me? What do you get from all of this?"

Nancy and I hadn't really discussed why we wanted to help Mary. We didn't need to. We just knew. It felt right.

"We want to help you, Mary, because we've both felt underappreciated," Nancy explained. "We've both felt like we, as women, weren't worth fighting for, that the people stepping all over us had the right to do so. We didn't like who we were because of those people. Kody hasn't told me a whole lot about you, but from what I've heard you say already this morning and from observing your body language, I can see for myself that you aren't happy."

Tears streamed down Mary's cheeks.

It was my turn. "I fully believe that if you can learn to love yourself again, you can be happy. It all begins with you. Like I've said before, you are in charge of your own happiness. You must take control of your life and live it the way you want. The days of letting your husband and stepdaughter walk all over you are over. Nancy and I want to help you get your life back on track."

"And what better way to do that than a makeover?" Nancy chimed in.

Silence filled the air. I wasn't sure if Mary was seriously considering our offer or trying to figure out an escape plan.

Placing her hands at her sides, Mary asked, "Do you really think I can be happy again?"

"I do," I said.

"I do too," Nancy agreed.

Not wanting to give her too much time to decide, I quickly asked, "Are you ready for this, Mary?"

A smile started to form on Mary's lips. "Yes…yes, I'm ready for this. It won't be easy and I don't know if it will change who I am, but for today it sounds like a lot of fun. I don't remember the last time someone did something this nice for me."

The three of us stood up joining together for a much needed group hug. Tears of appreciation spilled from Mary's eyes. I was even getting a little choked up. It wasn't every day I was able to help a woman get her life back. To me, this makeover was a simple fix meant to build self-esteem. To her, it was two people reaching out to show her they cared. Today wasn't going to fix the problems she had at home, but it was a start. No one should feel worthless and ugly.

After the tissue box was passed around and Nancy's makeup was once again picture perfect, Mary and Nancy departed for their first appointment at the spa and salon where they were scheduled to receive facials, massages, haircuts, and color. They begged me to reconsider joining them, but I told them I needed to stay behind to catch up on some work, which was partly true. I did have a few things I wanted to finish up. My main sticking point for not joining them was that I had a really hard time with people I didn't know touching me. The facial might have been okay, but the massage? No way. I didn't need some random person, or worse yet, someone I knew, rubbing all over me. It gave me the creeps just thinking about it. The back of my thighs were no one's business.

I lingered out in front of my office after watching Nancy's vehicle disappear from sight. The men next door were busily working on Sam's office and fortunately there was no sign of Sam. I soaked up as many rays of sunshine as I could before heading back in. Being a Minnesotan, you had to relish these days because come January and February a break in the gloomy weather was hard to come by. A day of sunshine was a cause for celebration.

"Kody," a male voice said from behind me.

I quickly turned around. When I saw who it was, I wished I had pretended not to hear him.

"Hi, Sam," was all I said. He didn't deserve anything more.

"Enjoying the beautiful weather we're having?"

Without answering, I turned to go inside. I wasn't about to sit out here and make small talk with him. He'd had enough chances to act like a civilized adult and had failed miserably each time.

"Kody, I'm really sorry about the other night," he said, moving to block my entrance.

"Please move," I said.

"I said I was sorry. Can you please forgive me? I feel terrible for the way I acted. That wasn't the real me. I'm not always that guy."

What the hell did he mean he wasn't always that guy? Why would he purposely choose to act that way if it wasn't the real him? Did he really believe "that guy" impressed people? Clearly he hadn't won me over.

"I guess I can forgive you, if that's what you want, but I'll never go out with you again. You, or whichever one of your personalities I was on a date with, need to learn how to treat a woman. I guarantee you I'm not the only woman in this town who doesn't appreciate being told she has good birthing hips."

"I know," he said, rubbing his hand on his forehead. "That was totally uncalled for."

Sam looked remorseful. He even looked a bit ashamed. That still didn't change how I felt about the guy. First impressions were hard to mess with.

"Sam, if you'll excuse me, I really do need to get inside."

"I would like to make it up to you somehow," he said, stepping aside.

"It's a little too late I'm afraid. The most we can be is neighbors. Let's leave it at that."

Before the door fully closed behind me, I heard him say, "Sure. That would be nice."

I didn't turn around.

With the office silent and no clients due to come in, I sat at my desk to get some work done. I tried, I really did. All I did was stare at the computer screen. My thoughts were elsewhere. Some days were like that. No matter how much stuff I needed to get done, it just wasn't going to happen. Good thing too because Kendall called.

"I just got off the phone with your mom. Why didn't you tell me Paul was back in town?" Kendall asked.

"Why were you on the phone with my mom?"

"I wanted that stuffed shell recipe from her. I thought I would make those this weekend when Jason's aunt and uncle come to visit. Have you seen him yet? Your mom mentioned he was going to stop by."

"I don't like you talking to my mother."

"So did he?"

"Yes, he came by last week. I didn't mention it because it's not a big deal."

"Not a big deal? The only guy you've ever loved is newly divorced and he intentionally stops by to visit you. Not a big deal? I think not, sister."

"I didn't love him."

"Yes, you did," she said without hesitation. "Was it good to see him again?"

"Kendall, it was nothing. Really. He said hello. I said hello. He left. There's nothing more to it. I wish I could say we stripped off each other's clothes and had heated sex on my office floor, but that's not what happened."

"Damn. That would have made for a better story."

"Did my mom also tell you that he's going to be working at his dad's hardware store? Another one of our classmates has come crawling back home."

"Of course she mentioned that. You're mom isn't one to leave out any details. That just means you'll get to see more of him when you go home."

"I don't often get sent to pick up items from the hardware store."

"Your mom will come up with something. She really liked Paul."

"Only because his mom was her hairstylist. My mother holds her hairstylist above everyone else."

"Not to pry or anything…"

"That's not like you."

"Stop, Kody. I was just going to ask if you would ever consider dating him again. I mean, as much as you'll deny it, you two were in love in high school. There's no other word to describe it. Maybe you could try to rekindle that fire."

I didn't know how to answer that question. Since seeing Paul the other day, I had thought about him a lot. Most of the memories were good ones actually. The week after our graduation was an especially good one. We spent almost a full week at Paul's grandparents' lake cabin, just the two of us. We had to tell a few lies to make it happen, but because our time together was limited neither of us felt too guilty. Our days were spent basking in the sun while occasionally paddling out to the middle of the lake to jump in and cool off. At night we drank cheap beer and watched really awful movies. I've always considered that week one of the best. I've also always considered it one of the worst. That was the week I attributed to ending our fairy-tale romance.

"You seem to forget that we broke up even before he left for college," I said. "We must not have been that in love."

"That's right. You said you lost interest in him. I never bought it though. I assumed you ended the relationship before it ended itself. Not many couples can make a long-distance relationship work, especially since he was going so far away."

"Yeah, I knew it wouldn't work," I said, my voice trailing off as I was transported back in time.

Sensing that my thoughts were back in high school and not on our conversation, Kendall gave me an excuse to get off the phone. That left me to reminisce some more on my own. Was it possible that after all these years of searching for the man of my dreams, I had once held a tight grip on him? Had fate brought Paul back home, back into my life, to give us one more chance at love? I was a firm believer in fate, but I couldn't help but question it this time. Like a bad storm, the damage might be too much to recover from.

* * * *

"Mary, you look astonishing!" I gasped as she and Nancy breezed into my office in the late afternoon.

"Doesn't she though?" Nancy added. "After we got her into some new clothes, it didn't take too much convincing for her to see that she's still a beautiful woman. She just needed to shed a few inches off her hair length, apply the right makeup, and dress in more modern clothing."

"She's right," Mary agreed. "I feel amazing, and ten years younger. I never knew I could look this good."

"I am so happy for you. You deserve to be this happy so don't forget it, especially when you go home today. Don't let anyone pull you back down. You got that?" I said.

Mary nodded in agreement, but her expression weakened. I wondered if the mention of her family might have that effect on her. Nancy and I exchanged glances. We both knew it was going to take more than a makeover to change Mary's perception of herself.

"Believe in yourself, Mary," Nancy started, her voice filled with genuine passion. "Demand respect. We didn't work this hard today to throw it all away so quickly. When your stepdaughter and husband come home later this evening, you need to be who you want to be, not what they've turned you into. That weak, undesirable woman isn't you any longer. Show them that you can stand up to them, that you aren't willing to take their bullying and lies any longer. Show them that you have the strength to walk away if they don't see the value you add to your family. Make them wonder if they can live their lives without you. Once you believe in yourself, Mary, and I mean truly believe, there's nothing you can't do."

With awe on our faces, Mary and I looked at our friend with pure amazement. Never before had I seen this side of Nancy. I knew she had a big heart, which was why I asked for her help in the first place, but I had no idea how well-spoken she was when it came to what she believed in. Although, given her troubled past, it was safe to assume that Nancy had received this same speech from someone who believed in her. Nancy was merely paying it forward.

"That was beautiful," I finally said. Mary nodded in agreement, still wiping tears from her eyes being careful not to wipe off her newly-applied makeup.

"It's what I believe," Nancy said, leaning in for a hug. She pulled Mary in too and the three of us held each other once again, clinging to the strength we formed together. And even though it was Mary who received the makeover today, we all felt its effects because positive energy was contagious, and we could all stand to have a little more of that.

"Well, ladies," Nancy said, pulling away first, "it's been a long, but wonderful day, and I'm absolutely exhausted."

"I should be going too," Mary said.

"You look beautiful, Mary, and I'm very proud of you for doing this. You didn't have to, you know."

"Yes, I did, Kody. I had to do this for myself."

"I'm glad to hear you say that because everyone deserves to be happy."

23

To: kodyburkoff@inyourwords.com
From: sad_dad1@gmail.com
Subject: I did it again

Got what they deserved. Of course they got what they deserved. They made poor Cinderella sleep with the animals while they slept in lavish bedding surrounded by beautiful possessions. She was repressed, unable to live the life deserving of her. The prince falling in love with her was her only way out. He broke poor Cinderella out of the prison she was living in. He gave her the freedoms sought by all others in the kingdom. The stepmother and stepsisters were left to wallow in their self-pity, knowing that their lives would be forever changed. We never find out if they were remorseful for their actions. We also never learn if Cinderella forgave them for their selfish ways.

That little bastard said he felt remorse for what happened to Julia. He said he never meant to hurt her. I never meant to kill my cat with a BB gun when I was a kid, but it happened. Kids don't always immediately reflect on their actions, but they need to own up to them. I confessed to killing the cat and I was punished by my parents. He should confess to killing my daughter and be punished by me.

The real reason I'm writing to you is because I did it again. I know you don't want to hear this since you told me how proud you were of me. I wish you had never said that. I'm no one to be proud of. Last night I went to his house again, only this time I didn't stay in the car. I needed to get closer. I crept close enough to hear the television and his mom asking him to turn the volume down. It was like I was a part of their family, only I wasn't.

My actions were triggered by a show I watched on television. It was *20/20* or some sort of investigative news program like that. I couldn't believe how much the story resembled my own. It was about an angry dad wishing to seek revenge on his child's alleged murderer who was running around free because there wasn't enough evidence to link the two together. The dad was basically stalking the guy. He was real nonchalant about it too. Long story short, the murderer committed suicide and left a note confessing to killing this guy's son along with several other children. What a spectacular ending! I can only hope the same happens in my case, not the multiple killing part because that is just sick. I'm talking about the part where the murderer commits suicide. Sure as hell would make my life a whole lot easier. You and I wouldn't even be having this conversation right now.

Anyway, I should have known those forward-thinking days wouldn't last. I can't stop who I've become. No one can. Not even you, Kody.

sad dad

24

"What do I do, Kendall?" I pleaded, sinking down farther under my covers. Every time I attempted to close my eyes I saw a murder happening. Since Kendall was a night owl despite having to get up early every morning, I called my friend to unload.

"I still can't believe you let it go this far, Kody! What were you thinking?"

"You know what I was thinking. I have a sickness. I'm impelled to help every lost soul that enters my life." Hearing the disappointment and disbelief in Kendall's voice made me burrow even deeper. What *was* I thinking? What was I trying to prove?

"Well, the first thing you need to do is stop e-mailing this guy. Hopefully he'll take the hint and go away."

"But I can't just leave him hanging. I have to tell him something. Plus, I already have pages put together from what he's sent me. Some of what he wrote was useful."

"Useful information from him is where he lives or works so you can give the police more information to work with. You need to call the police, you know."

"And what exactly do I tell them?" I asked, shuddering at the thought of having to explain my predicament. "That I've been receiving e-mails from a psychotic man who lives somewhere in the United States?"

"Well, we have his e-mail address. I bet with some digging we can come up with his location on our own."

"I tried that already. I didn't find anything."

"Then we need to find someone who can."

I knew exactly where this was going.

"You and I aren't computer geeks," she said, "but lucky for us we know a very good one. He's even good looking and still single. Bonus."

"Why is it that every time I get into a pinch, Kevin is the first person that comes to your mind?" I asked, sitting up in bed.

"I don't know. He's dependable. He's got a lot of useful skills, ones that we don't have, and he misses you. Every time I see him he asks about you."

"I don't want to get into that right now," I whined. "I'll think about it."

"What's there to think about? The quicker you wash your hands of this sad dad the better. And must I remind you that I'm going on vacation soon? I won't feel right leaving town until you're rid of this guy."

I really didn't want to include Kevin in this mess, but I understood Kendall's point. I also felt it in my gut that it was time to be rid of sad dad, which is why I called Kendall for help in the first place. Fortunately, so far in our conversation she hadn't said, "I told you so."

"Okay, I'll call him," I said with little enthusiasm. "I'll just send him sad dad's e-mail and we'll see what he can find out. Hopefully it will be enough to hand over to the police."

"That's the spirit. I think you're making a really good decision here, Kody."

"I'm going to send sad dad one final e-mail. He deserves that much. Part of me still feels sorry for the guy."

"Do what you need to do as long as he's out of your life and I can go on my vacation not having to worry about you."

"Got it, Kendall. I'll talk to you later."

"Let me know how it goes with Kevin."

"Yep."

"And Kody… I told you so," she said before ending the call.

"That was cheap," I yelled as I pulled the phone away from my ear.

I turned the lamp off and assumed the sprinter's position under the covers, hoping to keep my thoughts focused on the upcoming conversation I was going to have with Kevin instead of on the various ways sad dad might torture and then murder his daughter's killer. It was no use. Within seconds of me closing my eyes, my mind was corrupted by visions of death and gore. My brain couldn't spit out the answer to a trivia question, but it sure could whip up a murder scene in no time flat. What was I going to do? How was I ever going to get some sleep?

Unable to clear my mind, I wrapped up in my bathrobe and plopped down at the computer. Perhaps if I wrote my final message to sad dad I would be able to get some rest. That was one item on my checklist. Unfortunately, after a quick glance through my Inbox, I wished I had stayed in bed. Whatever nightmare I was going to have tonight, couldn't compare to the nightmare revealing itself in real life.

To: kodyburkoff@inyourwords.com
From: sad_dad1@gmail.com
Subject: I hate him too

I hate him too. He ruined my life. Every time I see him at the movie theater or playing basketball at the park downtown with his friends I get really angry, almost as angry as my dad. My dad doesn't know this, but we have more in common than he thinks.

Things at home were never great, but they sure were better before Julia died. Her death only accentuated all that was wrong with our family. We stayed together and made it work though. We all put some effort into keeping things running smoothly. Well, Dad and I kept our distance, which was for the best, while he and my mom swooned over Julia. Julia was the one that forced us all to get along. She stuck up for me when Dad and I got into an argument. She invited me to go places when both of my parents thought it was best to leave me alone. I like being alone. I've always preferred it actually, which kind of freaks people out sometimes. But when Julia was with me, I felt okay.

My mom tries to understand. My dad doesn't get it at all. He still forces me to go places, just the two of us. It never turns out well. I put up an imaginary wall between us because I'm not who he wants me to be. I never have been. I don't ever plan on being the son he's always wanted. It frustrates him that I'm not more like his favorite child, Julia. What can I say? I've always been more like him. He just doesn't see it.

Julia thrived on people looking at her. The more attention she got, the happier it made her feel. Unfortunately, her attention-seeking ways was what probably got her killed. She wanted that guy's attention. From what I've overheard at school, she was forcing herself on him. He could have made that up though to look less guilty. There were plenty of rumors going around at school about what really happened that day at the campground. I still don't know what to believe. I have one parent who has already forgiven the guy, accepting that the whole thing was an accident, and the other one who is ready to commit murder when the timing is right.

Dad isn't the only one who wants to see that guy get what's coming to him. Our family is totally different now because of what happened. My parents are no longer married. My mom is sad most of the time because she doesn't know what to be happy about. I try to put a smile on her face by doing well in school. It doesn't help much though. Her eyes seem empty when I talk to her. It's like she doesn't see me. Something was stolen from her the day Julia died. Something was stolen from all of us.

I followed my dad to the guy's house the other night. When he was pulling out of the driveway, I left through the back door. I cut through yards to keep up with him. He didn't go far. He didn't need to. I had predicted where he was headed anyway. A small part of me thought, even hoped, that he was sneaking off to see a woman. That would have meant he was moving on. No such luck. Instead, he parked just down the street from the guy's house. I watched as he turned off the headlights and then waited a few minutes before getting out of the car.

It was only eleven o'clock and there were still lights on in the house so I knew someone was awake watching TV or something. My dad, bent over trying to remain as low as possible, ran from his car to the lilac bush at the corner of the house. He was right next to the large window in their living room. I couldn't believe how risky he was being. It's like he wasn't afraid of getting caught. He stuck his head around the bush and stayed there for at least ten minutes. It seemed longer. After he was done, he ran back to the car and just sat there.

I didn't want to stick around to see what happened next so I ran as fast as I could back home. I went into my bedroom, locked the door, and turned up the music as loud as it would go, wishing for it all to be over. I couldn't help but think that if my dad wasn't man enough to put an end to our misery, I would be forced to do it for us. Someone needed to take control of this family.

The message wasn't signed. It didn't need to be. The e-mail came from sad dad's account, most likely from his home, but it wasn't from him. It was Gabe. Why was he e-mailing me? Did he want to scare me or was it a cry for help? Did he want me to hear his side of the story? There were too many questions that I couldn't answer. It was time to call in for backup. I needed to get the ball rolling or there was going to be an even bigger tragedy to recover from: a murder with two suspects.

Kevin answered on the third ring.

"I know it's late, but I need your help," I said.

"Who is this? Kody, is that you?"

"Yes, it's me. Have you forgotten my voice already?"

"I would never forget your voice. Are you in trouble? Where are you?" he asked, obviously surprised by my late night call. "I can be there in five minutes."

"Kevin, I'm not in any trouble. Not yet anyway. I'm at home. I can't sleep though because I've got myself in the middle of something that I was hoping you could help get me out of."

I explained my predicament. As I spoke, I pictured my blond-haired, blue-eyed ex-boyfriend staring intently at the stark-white walls of his bedroom. He was also probably running his forever-cold fingers through his hair. I always thought that was sexy.

"Wow, that's one hell of a story. I'll try to help you. I can't make any promises though."

"Just try, Kevin. That's all I can ask."

My emotions ran high as I read to Kevin sad dad's last e-mail, and then his son's, solidifying the real danger I was tangled in. My voice wavered as I finished reading the words on the screen. I felt weak, vulnerable, and alone, much like how sad dad and his son must feel on a daily basis. I didn't want to have that in common with them. I didn't want to have anything in common with them. I desperately wanted a warm body next to me, someone to listen to my fears, someone to make everything all better.

"Kody, are you going to be okay?"

"I don't know," I said, my voice barely above a whisper.

"Do you want me to come over? You sound like you could use a friend."

Before I had time to logically think through my answer, I heard myself say yes.

"I'll be there in five minutes."

25

Waking up to the alarm was expected. Waking up naked in Kevin's arms was not. How easily I forgot that I had finally fallen asleep last night out of pure exhaustion, both mental and physical. As I wiped the sleep from my eyes, I recalled the night's events: reading the son's e-mail, calling Kevin, Kevin coming to my rescue, me talking in circles, Kevin and me making love. The last event was not planned. Hell, none of it was planned. Never in a million years did I expect to hear from sad dad's son and feel just as creeped out by his words. Like father, like son.

Not wanting to wake my bed companion, I gently slipped from his embrace, tiptoed over the clothes strewn about, and grabbed my bathrobe from the closet. Kevin and I couldn't get our clothes off fast enough when the mood hit us last night. It was all a blur. One minute he was sitting next to me listing off the various ways to research sad dad's e-mail address, the next minute I was laying on top of him kissing him like a ravaged lioness. It was me! I started it! I don't know if it was the lack of sleep or what, but I pounced on that man demanding to be pleasured like he'd done so many times before.

"Kody," Kevin murmured from the comforts of my bed. "Are you feeling better?"

I gave him a dirty look because now I knew that he had watched me walk naked across the room and because I didn't know where he was going with that question.

"I mean about the e-mails," he added.

"I think so," I said with jaded confidence. "I think I know what to do. You'll work on your part today?"

"I promised, didn't I?" he said.

Even though I was satisfied with his response, I ordered him out of bed. He was expected at work by eight o'clock and it was already seven thirty.

"I'm leaving," he said with disappointment in his voice. "It's too bad we can't just lie in bed all day. I can call in sick and you can," he paused, "you can not show up for work and we'll watch all those episodes of *CSI* you have on your DVR."

"You just promised me you would work on the e-mail address. I have an e-mail to write." Biting my tongue on what was set to come out next, I left the room. I almost said that just because we had sex last night, it didn't mean we were getting back together. That wasn't very polite to say to someone while they're lying in your bed, especially when they got out of their bed to come to your rescue. I would have to think about how to deal with Kevin now that he was back in my life. It was comforting to have him here with me though. He didn't judge me when I told him how my relationship with sad dad got started, which was more than I could say for Kendall. Kevin listened intently, offering suggestions only when I asked for his opinion. And when I mauled him, he quickly retreated without any questions asked.

Kevin was fully clothed when he joined me in the kitchen. He leaned against the refrigerator, waiting for me to look up from the newspaper article I was staring at. Who could read at a time like this?

When I finally lowered the newspaper to meet his hungry stare, he said, "I'm glad you called me last night."

With a smirk, I answered, "I'm glad you were able to calm me down."

Kevin closed the gap between us. Hesitant to lift his hopes any higher, or mine for that matter, I instinctively raised my chin to receive his kiss. It was as sweet and gentle as only hours before when we allowed our bodies to relish in the feeling of satisfaction.

That sealed it. I had just opened a can of worms I wasn't ready to fish with.

* * * *

"She did it!"

"Who did what?" I asked Anna when she called later that morning.

"Hermione peed in the toilet all by herself."

Anna was clearly excited about her cat's accomplishment. I still thought it was weird. My cat, Percy, and I had an understanding that we did our business in separate rooms. Plus, the odds of me finding a husband would decrease tremendously if the guy found out I shared a toilet with my cat. Can you say creepy cat lady?

"That's great news, Anna."

"I know. When can you come over?"

"Um, I don't know," I said. I should have said I'd be right over. When else was I going to be asked to watch a cat pee in a toilet? I heard Brian's voice interrupt Anna's next comment, and then I heard Anna whine, "But, Dad."

"Sorry about that, Kody," Brian said, commandeering the phone. "This obsession she has with that toilet seat is driving Ethan and me crazy. There's no need for you to get involved too."

"Oh, I don't mind. You have to admit, it is pretty cool."

Brian hesitated. "You can come over for dinner tonight if you want to witness the spectacle."

Thinking fast on my feet, I lied, "I have plans already tonight. Maybe another night. Thanks for the offer though."

"Sure, maybe another night," he said, sounding disappointed.

Complicating my life even further by adding Brian to the mix was not something I wanted to do. I cared too much about him and his family to eventually hurt his feelings.

As soon as I put the phone down, Mrs. Lopez walked through my door holding on to Princess. I should have expected as much. It had been almost a week since her last visit. A lot can happen in one week, especially for her. Her life was way more exciting than mine. She was involved in this and that, and then she had an endless number of lunch and dinner dates. Mrs. Lopez was a very likeable, loveable woman so it didn't surprise me that she was so popular.

"Kody, darling. How are you this fine morning?"

"Apparently not as good as you," I said. "I'm still drinking coffee. You, on the other hand, look like you just stepped out of a wonderful dream."

Mrs. Lopez blushed, appearing embarrassed that I noticed this about her.

"Please, do tell," I demanded.

"Emil," escaped her lips. Assuming she was gathering the rest of her thoughts, I poured us each a fresh cup of coffee. I set them on the sunny table up front.

"He's the guitar player I told you about last week," she said, sitting down in the chair I motioned for her to take. "The man from the farmer's market?"

"Oh, yes, of course. Did you see him again? Was he playing somewhere else?"

"Well, I more than just saw him."

"Mrs. Lopez! I didn't think you had it in you," I joked.

"Oh, Kody," she said, shaking her head. "We merely ate together. You know I would never do anything like that."

"I'm only teasing. Go ahead. Tell me about Emil."

"Yesterday we ate lunch and dinner together. I'll get to the story in a second, but first I must tell you that he is just about the nicest, sweetest man I have met in a very long time. When he smiles, I smile too. When he tells funny stories, they're actually funny. When he

129

talks about his children and grandchildren, his eyes sparkle. He truly is one of those people you feel lucky to meet."

Young love. Or was it old, young love? Did it really matter?

"He must really be something. I'm curious to know where you ran into him again."

"I was having lunch with a dear friend of mine at Donna's. You know that place owned by the woman who lost her left arm in a farming accident? Bless her heart. It must be so hard. Anyway, my friend had to leave early for an appointment so I sat alone finishing up my coffee. I always like to have one cup of coffee after a meal. Well, I looked over at another table and there was Emil sitting all by his lonesome. Moments later he was sitting at my table with me. He said I looked like I would be good company."

"You are good company," I agreed. "I bet he was also feeling pretty lucky to be sharing a table with such a beautiful woman."

"You are too much today. What's come over you?"

"I don't know," I smirked. I could have told her about the crazy turn of events last night, but I knew she wouldn't approve of my indiscretion. "So, you hit it off so well that you decided to have dinner together too? I can't even pull that off. One meal with me and they're ready to run," I joked.

"It doesn't have to be like that, you know. You're part of the problem, if you don't mind me saying so."

Whoa. Keep the gloves up. Here I was shelling out compliments and she chose to point out my flaws. I preferred to hear blatant honesty from my mother or Kendall. That was it.

"Actually, I do mind you saying so, but let's continue our conversation about you and Emil."

Why was it that everyone assumed it was my problem that I couldn't find a suitable man? Did it ever occur to them that there were no glimmering fish in the sea, that the sea was filled with those annoying sunfish that jumped on the hook as soon as you threw your line in? Where were the big, ol' bass or the shiny walleyes, the ones you saw jumping just out of reach of your cast? Why weren't they swimming in closer? What were they afraid of? I wasn't going to fillet them or leave them in a cooler too long to die. I knew how to treat a fish. I was sure Kevin felt like a stealthy salmon this morning.

As if nothing hurtful was ever said, Mrs. Lopez continued. "Emil invited me over to his house for dinner, which I was unsure about at first. I barely knew the man. Like I've heard you say before, he could have been a serial rapist for all I knew. I took the chance though and I'm glad I did. He's a wonderful cook. Eduardo was a terrible cook. He couldn't even make rice that was edible."

"Eduardo probably did it on purpose so that you would do all the cooking."

"You know, you're probably right."

Mrs. Lopez's joyful disposition turned to sadness.

"I didn't think I would ever find love again after Eduardo died. I know Emil and I spent less than a day together, but it was just perfect. He's perfect."

"Love at first sight," I mumbled under my breath.

"What did you say, Kody?"

"I said, 'Love at first sight.' Yesterday, you experienced it. You experienced what I've been searching for since puberty."

"How can that be? I'm an old woman. I've experienced love plenty of times. I was married to a wonderful man."

"Has it ever been so immediate though? Have you ever felt like you've known a person your whole life and only just met them?"

She pondered my question.

I was too in awe of the situation to even be jealous.

"Kody, I see where you're coming from, but have you considered that at the ripe old age of seventy-nine I know what makes my ticker pound a little faster? I know by now which qualities in a man I enjoy and which ones I don't. Emil just so happens to have the bright eyes of a wise man who has lived a lot of life. He has the smile of someone who has loved before and has been loved in return. He also has a kind heart that tells me he is a good friend and neighbor. Those were the qualities that immediately struck me yesterday."

"But…" I began.

"I think when you're young, love looks different. It's more superficial. Yes, Emil is a handsome man, even at eighty-three, but that's not what I find so endearing about him. I can close my eyes, only to hear his voice and the music he plays on his guitar, and still be fond of him. Love at first sight isn't necessarily something I believe in. Love for the everlasting is what we should all be striving for."

I didn't have an immediate response. Those words could only be spoken by a woman who has experienced love, loss, and everything in between.

"He reminds me of Eduardo in many ways," Mrs. Lopez continued. "Eduardo used to close his eyes and say a prayer before each meal. Emil did that yesterday. Eduardo kept a hankie in his back pocket. I noticed Emil pull one out of his pocket after tears of joy welled in his eyes. He told me a funny story about his oldest daughter and her daughter. It was similar to something we had both experienced while raising our own children. Some things in life never change."

"How true," I said.

"Oh, I never told you what we did between meals."

"He fanned you and fed you grapes on your back deck?"

"Not quite," she said, rolling her eyes. "Emil took me to play bingo at the senior citizen center. I don't usually like to go there. There's nothing but a bunch of old people complaining about their ailments. Emil insisted though and it didn't end up being as bad as I thought. I even won a few times."

"Do they play for cash? I'm looking for a way to earn some extra money."

"Goodness, Kody," she sighed.

"I know. I'm being slightly intolerable today."

"That's fine. I should be going anyway," she said, getting up from her chair.

"Thanks for sharing your story. I know it's for your memoir, but I always end up taking something away from our conversations."

"I just hope I gave you a little lesson in love."

"I'm all the wiser for having you in my life."

26

To: sad_dad1@gmail.com
From: kodyburkoff@inyourwords.com
Subject: It's time to seek help

Dear sad dad,

I no longer believe that our working relationship is what's best for your well-being. I highly suggest you seek help from either a therapist or someone else you feel comfortable talking to about the feelings you are having. There are times when I see a breakthrough in you, but more often than not your thoughts are consumed with what remains out of your control. You cannot control the past. Nothing you do now will ever bring Julia back to you. Any harmful actions you think will justify the past are only going to make things worse. You run the risk of never seeing your son become a man, or worse yet, of not growing old in the comforts of your own home. It would be a shame to spend the rest of your life behind bars.

I worry about you. I worry about the life you are choosing to live. There must be a better way and there must be a reason to get out of bed each morning. Find that reason, that purpose. Is it the hope that you'll one day have a good relationship with your son? If not that, then there must be something or someone else worth living for. Julia would have wanted you to be happy. She would have wanted you to be successful, to live life to its fullest. No, she didn't get that chance, which is truly unfortunate, but you have it. You have the chance to make her proud. You have the chance to show those around you that you can pick yourself up after feeling the worst kind of devastation and continue on with your life. This should be your focus. This alone should be the reason you get out of bed each morning.

With that said, I'll keep what we've worked on thus far. I don't think reading through the memories this soon will help you any. Maybe sometime in the future when you're feeling up to it, we can attempt this again. Maybe sometime in the future you'll find happiness in the past.

All the best,
Kody

27

Sad dad's e-mail was the last message I wrote before driving over to meet the garden gals. I second-guessed my words the entire drive. Whatever it was I thought I was doing for this man, it wasn't working. His messages still included deranged thoughts, thoughts that most people didn't have, or at least didn't type out for fear of leaving a paper trail. Sad dad didn't care though. He didn't care that he was telling me, a perfect stranger, that he wanted to kill someone. He didn't care who saw him staked out in front of that poor kid's house. You can't tell me this kid's parents didn't know he was out there. They had to know. If my thoughts were correct, then why did they let it continue? Why didn't they call the police and have him arrested?

Turning around the last bend, I felt my face light up at the vision of green blotted with bright, big bottoms poking up into the air like dandelions in a well-manicured lawn. There was something to be said about surrounding yourself with nature. It somehow blanketed me with calmness, which in turn made the stresses of daily life vanish.

Marjie was the first to greet me.

"I learned something about that murder you were asking about last week," she said.

So much for the blanket of calmness.

"You did?" I asked. "What did you find out?"

Marjie motioned for me to follow her over to one of the picnic tables covered with sweets and Styrofoam cups that were once filled with hot coffee. I purposely arrived late so that I would miss the chit-chat session where everyone indulged in the baked goods sitting on the table. I knew better than to entice myself. It was swimsuit season and every lemon bar and fig cookie counted.

"I don't want to upset anyone. Hearing about violence can be awfully upsetting for some of them, you know."

I nodded. I was eager for her to continue.

"Well, I went to my daughter's house last weekend. My granddaughter had a small role in the community's production of *Our Town*. She was only an extra body in the background, but I would have never heard the end of it if I had missed the performance. My daughter is real particular about things like that. One year I took a cruise during my other granddaughter's dance recital and my Lanie didn't talk to me for months. She forgets that I have a life too. My life doesn't revolve around those little girls like hers does. Oh, I'd never tell her that. She makes it very clear that she's a career woman who can do it all. Ha! I've yet to meet a woman who can do it all."

Marjie paused and leaned in closer. "You want to hear about the murder, right?"

Before I had a chance to reply, she continued, "I can ramble on for hours. Everyone tells me that, you know. I'll never forget the time I was visiting my brother out in San Diego, California. What a beautiful place that is. The sandy beaches, palm trees, and warm ocean breezes were enough to make me consider moving. I could never leave here though. This is my home. I take care of my mother and she…"

She lost me is what she did. While Marjie further convinced me that it was easy for her to ramble on for hours, I kept my patience intact by checking out my gardening competition. As usual, Gertie had us beat. I didn't know what she did to those plants, but they always looked a little more bountiful than the rest of ours. I would have to make sure to pick my plot next to hers next year.

"It was in Bergan. The murder."

Marjie again had my attention.

"I was on the phone talking to an old friend of mine from high school when something she said triggered me to ask her about the murder you had mentioned. She said it was such a tragedy because the girl, Julia, was a wonderful student with a bright future. It's always hard to hear about a young person's death. Anyway, it tore the family to pieces. Julia's father, Michael Calhoun, never went back to his teaching job at the elementary school. I guess he rarely leaves his house now, and when he does he looks terrible. That's what my friend said at least. She thought the couple had a son too but she didn't know anything about him. The mother still works at the bank."

Marjie's story seemed to match up. Julia. Broken family. Elementary school—sad dad had mentioned school at least once before. A son.

"You're awesome, Marjie," I said, giving her a big hug. "I can't tell you how happy I am to have that information."

"You're very welcome. I'm glad I could help. You know…"

"Marjie," I said before she got started again, "I really need to check on my garden before getting back to the office. Thanks again."

Excited to share the news with Kevin and to tell him I beat him to the punch, I jogged over to my plot, said hello to the other ladies along the way, and quickly inspected my produce. I didn't bother to pull a single weed before making the call.

"I'm glad you called. I know who sad dad is," Kevin said.

"So do I."

"What do you mean? How could you? It was a pain in the ass going through all the hoops I did. I even owe one guy lunch."

"Sorry. I only needed to do some gardening."

"Figures. So you know Michael Calhoun lives in Bergan then. That's only about two hundred miles away."

"Yeah, I know," I said, still unable to believe how well everything was working out. Now that I had the information I needed, all that was left to do was call the Bergan police department and explain the situation. It was going to be tricky because sad dad, I mean Michael Calhoun, hadn't technically done anything wrong, although I was fairly certain it was illegal to stand outside someone's window and gawk at them. That's like a peeping tom or something.

"You're going to call the police, right? That's what the next step was," Kevin said.

"Yep…that's the next step."

Hearing my hesitation, Kevin said, "Don't make me rat you out to Kendall. Calling the police is the right thing to do, Kody. You can't protect this guy anymore. After talking with you last night, I thought that's what you wanted, to be rid of him."

Quickly coming to my senses, I said, "It is what I want. You're right. I'll call the police as soon as I get back to the office."

"I'm going to hold you to that. How about you give me the details over dinner?"

I knew that was coming.

"Kevin, I know last night was crazy and totally unexpected."

"It was amazing, Kody. It felt right holding you again."

"I don't want you to assume that we're back together again though."

"I'm not assuming anything. I was just hoping you would have dinner with me tonight. You never know, maybe this is our chance to give it another try."

Logically it made sense. Maybe we were meant to have a second chance. Maybe fate was trying to tell us both something. I mean, obviously, there was some chemistry going on between us last night or else I never would have attacked him like I did. My actions still boggled me.

"Okay, I'll have dinner with you," I said, feeling that nervous energy inside. My mind took that as a cue that the heart had made a good decision.

"I knew you would say yes."

"No, you didn't. You were sweating bullets just now."

"Nope. I know you can't deny all that I have to offer."

I laughed.

"Okay, Romeo. We could do this for hours. Pick me up at six thirty?"

"I'm there."

* * * *

Back at the office, I researched Julia's death by reading everything relevant to the case, which led me to the name of the boy Michael and his son were stalking: Peder Knutson. Peder was about to enter his senior year in high school making him two years younger than Julia. I located the previous year's football team picture in the newspaper archives. He was a good-looking kid. I could see why Julia wanted to get to know him.

The newspaper didn't offer up too many more details about the accident other than what I had already learned from Michael. I also searched on Michael's name figuring with what Marjie had told me and with what I already knew about him, the Knutson family might have slapped a restraining order on him. My search came up empty. Michael was only mentioned in conjunction with school activities.

Satisfied that I had hit on every angle in the search criteria, I did some organizing and created a folder to hold the e-mail exchanges between Michael and me. I wanted to be prepared for when I talked to the Bergan police so that I didn't sound like a complete lunatic. Plus, I knew they would want me to forward them the proof that I had gathered. Doing so was probably against my confidentiality practices, but I figured it was worth doing if it was a chance to save someone's life.

Not wanting to prolong the inevitable, I dialed the number. And from the incident with Daniel last winter, I knew to speak to an investigator right off the bat.

"That's some story," Investigator Dunn said after I gave him a brief summary. "How long has this been going on?"

"Only a couple of weeks. I really thought I could help this man."

"I'm sure you did. Have you called the Knutson family?"

"No. I thought that might be something you would want to do."

"Yes, of course. We'll take care of that. We'll also pay Michael a visit to see how he's doing. I actually knew him back in high school. It's a shame what happened to his daughter. I heard he was still having a hard time with her death, but this goes beyond the normal grieving process. My wife works with his wife, I mean ex-wife. Julia's death took a toll on their marriage. Most marriages can't hold up to that kind of loss."

"Are you going to mention my name when you see him? Our conversations were supposed to be confidential and I don't think he would appreciate me coming to you. I just didn't want things to escalate any further. Michael isn't well. He's not thinking straight."

"I agree with you there. I'll keep you out of it as best I can."

Dunn asked me to forward the e-mails as I had suspected. He also asked that I refrain from any further communication with Michael. I didn't mention the e-mail I had sent earlier in the day.

"You don't know Michael's mindset," he added. "If he feels comfortable talking to you, he may not want to stop. All you can do is not reply."

"Right. Okay, so I guess you're going to take care of everything and I'm done with this whole mess."

"I'll get in touch with you if I have any questions," he said before asking for my contact information. "Is there anything else I can help you with?"

"Yes, actually there is. When you visit Michael, will you check out what kind of vehicle he drives and get back to me? Someone parked in my driveway the other night and I'm still trying to figure out who it was."

"I can do that. I'll let you know."

Why not kill two birds with one stone? By ruling out Michael as my uninvited guest on Saturday night, I'll feel a little safer and maybe be able to stave off those awful nightmares I've been having. No one deserves to have visions of death and gore when they should be having visions of jumping sheep. Come to think of it, I'd rather not be thinking about sheep. And where did that come from anyway? Who in the world came up with the idea to envision fluffy, white sheep jumping over a white picket fence to get relaxed?

28

To: kodyburkoff@inyourwords.com
From: sad_dad1@gmail.com
Subject: You can't quit

I know you don't want to work with me anymore. I can't blame you. Most days I don't want to be with me anymore either. My mind isn't working quite like it should. I'm not always making the best decisions. What little steam I had left is quickly running out, if you hadn't already caught on to that. This whole thing, living with grief, is harder than I thought. I had hoped these memories might put me in a better place, take me back to a time when all was right with the world: my family was complete, my career was following its course, and I was loved. Instead, remembering the days of long ago makes me miss her more. I miss her so much. But more than anything, I miss the life I used to have. It wasn't perfect by any means, but it sure as hell was better than being alone most nights eating whatever was in the freezer.

I want to accept what happened to Julia. I want to forgive the boy who was involved. I want to make amends with my son. It's so hard. The anger I have built up inside of me is too powerful. It blinds me with its fury. Sometimes I wonder if there's something seriously wrong with me. I was sane before Julia's death. I didn't need medication to fall asleep. I didn't need prescription drugs to control my rage. Everything is different now. My life, to put it plainly, sucks. I have nothing to live for. I have no one to live for. Maybe my compulsion to kill is aimed at the wrong person. Wouldn't that be something?

sad dad

29

"Who are the flowers from?" Mary asked after we sat down with our cups of coffee. It was nearing lunch time, but I needed a little pick-me-up. Some days were like that.

"They're from my date last night. It wasn't necessary. We've dated before."

"I think it's nice. He wants you to know he's thinking of you. There's nothing wrong with that. You should consider yourself lucky."

Her kind words were spoken with a solemn face, which made me wonder how her big reveal went at home after her exciting day with Nancy. From the looks of it, all from that day had been quickly forgotten. She wore the same boring clothes from before and not a smidge of makeup adorned her plain face.

"I should, I know. I'm still not sure what I want. Kevin and I broke up not too long ago because I hated our constant bickering and his predictability. Last night was great and we got along really well, but I can't help but wonder how long it will last before we pick up right where we left off."

"I know exactly what you mean," Mary said, running her hands through her hair. "When I got home the other afternoon after a wonderful day with you and Nancy, my family was incredibly excited for me. They loved my new look. They even told me I looked beautiful, and let me tell you, it has been a long time since I have heard those words. My husband even suggested we go out for dinner, which floored me because it has been months since we went anywhere in public together. It felt like what a normal family should feel like."

"That's great, Mary. Are you worried about how long it will last?"

"It's already over, Kody. The very next day everything was back to the way it was before. Stacy was her usual bitchy self and Mark told me he wouldn't be home for supper. When I asked him if he had a meeting, his reply was, 'Yeah, something like that.' All that work Nancy did was destroyed in less than twenty-four hours. Amazing, isn't it?"

Amazing was climbing to the top of Mount Everest or seeing the pyramids in Egypt. Cruel was a better word to describe Mary's situation. She was trying to change, but change was hard when those around you weren't willing to change too. A recovering alcoholic can't go into the same bar with his same friends and expect them to act any differently. If Mary truly wanted to make a lifestyle change, her environment needed to change as well.

"You know, it wasn't Nancy who did the work. That was all you. You're the one who chose to take the opportunity to better yourself. You didn't have to. You could have simply told us to mind our own business and kept on with your life as unhappy as you make it sound."

"I am unhappy. I wasn't for a few hours the other day though. For those few hours I was on top of the world. I felt like the old me, the girl that could step out on stage without a care in the world. The girl that felt beautiful and confident. The girl..."

"Can I ask you something?" I asked, rudely interrupting.

Mary nodded.

"Why do you stay?"

"What do you mean? I'm married. Married couples stay together," she said, sounding almost angry.

"Okay" was all I said. Her reaction led me to believe that that line of questioning was not open for discussion. Leaving her husband was not an option. I walked over to my desk to grab the newspaper clipping I had cut out from yesterday's paper. I placed it in front of her. "I thought you might be interested in this."

I watched her eyebrows inch up as she read the print.

"Are you?" I asked.

"Am I interested?"

"Yeah."

"It's been so long. I don't know if I could."

"Mary, you came to me. No, wait. You were referred to me by a doctor to help you rediscover the joy that life can bring. Now, I haven't known you for very long, but what you have shared with me is that you have a love for the theater. It's what makes you happy. Tell me you'll at least consider it."

Still holding the paper in her hand, she smiled weakly and said, "I'll think about it."

"Good. All the details are there. Auditions start tonight. Your husband won't be home anyway." I reached for her hand before continuing. "What have you got to lose?"

"I have nothing left to lose."

After Mary left with the community theater's audition schedule still in her grip, I checked my e-mail with the hopes of finding a few more interested clients. I didn't like how I was becoming more of a lifestyle coach than a ghostwriter. I surely wasn't qualified for the position, nor did I feel comfortable giving out advice. Well, actually I didn't mind handing out advice, solicited or not, I just didn't want to do it for a living.

One inquiry came in from a woman who lived in town. She was the sister of the librarian whom I had got to know rather well over the years. It probably wouldn't be the most exciting memoir I ever helped to write, but you never can tell. It was usually the ones you least expected to be naughty that surprised you. The preacher's wife had a few tales that were less than holy. She only met with me a few times before her conscience got the best of her. The story that sent her out the door for the last time was about the time when she ran away from home with her cousin, Frankie. They camped out in the woods for one night before surrendering to their folks. Now, I can assume a lot of things being that she walked out all red-faced, but that would send me straight to hell I figure. Instead, I placed a lock on my imagination and tried to put it out of my mind. It was incredibly hard though. I hated to leave a story unfinished.

Unfortunately, there was also another new message in my Inbox. It was from Michael. I had already forwarded his earlier e-mail to Investigator Dunn telling him that I had no intention of sending a reply even though Michael's final words still lingered in my thoughts. I considered passing along this message without reading it first, but in the end my curiosity got the best of me.

To: kodyburkoff@inyourwords.com
From: sad_dad1@gmail.com
Subject: He's worse than before

Way to go. My dad is worse than before. You really have no idea what you're doing, do you? You don't know what you got yourself into. I should have warned you earlier, but a small part of me thought that having him talk to you might help. A part of me also liked reading the e-mails he sent you about what Julia was like as a kid. He even mentioned my name a time or two, which was surprising.

I followed my dad again last night. He drove to the guy's house, which was no big surprise. It was almost two in the morning when I heard the garage door open. I slept in my clothes so it didn't take much for me to get out of bed and out the door. From the way he acted at supper, I knew something was up.

All the lights in their house were off. The whole neighborhood was dark. I lied down behind a big pine tree keeping an eye on both my dad and the sky. I didn't do a very good job because the sound of a car door closing woke me up. That's when I watched my dad creep up to the house again.

I followed him through the neighbor's backyard to the west side of the house. I moved slowly, keeping a safe enough distance between us. Finally, my dad stopped and crouched beneath a window. His back was to me. I didn't dare move a muscle, not even when he pulled out the gun he had brought with him. I had seen the gun before, but he always kept it locked in the glove compartment for whatever reason. Maybe this had been his reason the whole time.

The guy's bedroom window was open so the wire screen was the only separation between my dad and his target. Like my dad, I had done my due diligence. I probably knew more about this house than he did. I also knew that there was no security system and they didn't have a dog.

As I hid behind a bush, I wished for my dad to have the guts to pull the trigger. I wished for that asshole to get what he deserved. I didn't have the balls to do it, so who better to right the wrong than my own father. He deserved to watch this guy die. That piece of shit laying all snug in his bed had everything my poor sister didn't. He had things I no longer had. If Julia were still alive, our family would be together. I would still be in her shadow, but that was better than being referred to as "that dead girl's brother."

The sound of a door slamming put us both on alert. I stayed put while my dad shoved the gun down the back of his jean shorts and took off running through the neighbor's yard. A dog barked briefly and then all was silent. Not wanting to stick around to explain why I was hiding in someone's bush, I quietly crept away the same way I came. When I got to the sidewalk, I looked back at the house. That's when I saw someone standing in the front yard smoking a cigarette. It had to have been the guy's dad. I don't know if we woke him up or if he always got up in the middle of the night to have a smoke. I'm worried now though. What if he knows what my dad's been doing? What if he's like my dad and is waiting for the right moment to strike?

You need to fix this.

I immediately dialed Investigator Dunn's number.

"I just received another e-mail from the son. I demand that you tell me what you're doing to work on this case," I said.

"Hang on there, Ms. Burkoff. First off, this isn't a case and this also isn't one of those hour-long drama shows you watch at home."

What the hell did that mean? Not caring to hear an explanation, I continued, "Did you visit Michael Calhoun? Was his son there with him?"

"Yes, I visited Michael," he said calmly. "I asked him how he was doing and if he had been near the Knutson household. He told me he was feeling better and was working toward forgiving Peder. And no, his son was at his mother's at the time."

"That's crazy and you know it," I said, thinking about Michael forgiving Peder. "You read those e-mails. He's nowhere near forgiveness."

"I'm only telling you what he said. I didn't say I believed him."

"Well, that's a relief because the e-mail I'm forwarding to you now will make you even more of a nonbeliever. Michael's son, Gabe, was a busy boy this morning typing up a play-by-play of last night's escapade. It's disturbing to say the least. Michael took it one step further this time and Gabe was there watching in the shadows. They're like some sort of sick father-son duo."

"I'll take a look at it."

Completely irritated by Dunn's laissez-faire attitude, I continued with my questioning. Someone needed to light a fire under his ass and I was feeling up to the task. "Did you ask the Knutson family if they had been bothered by Michael recently? Were they aware that he was sitting outside their window at night?"

"I briefly spoke with Mr. Knutson about the possibility that Michael had been to his house on more than one occasion. His reaction surprised me I have to admit. He wasn't shocked by the news, at least not outwardly, and he didn't even ask me how I came up with the information. He said that his family felt sorry for the Calhoun's and hoped that they were all on the path to recovery." Dunn hesitated. "Then he told me to get off his property because the police department was of no use to him. He said he was fully capable of protecting his own family."

"That's interesting," I said, my voice raising an octave.

"Don't read anything into it. Some folks are like that. I've met more than my fair share."

"I'm sure you have. Did the wife ever do anything? Has there ever been a restraining order put on Michael?"

"Immediately after the accident, the Knutson's, assumingly the wife, filed for a restraining order. I wasn't working the case then so I don't personally know how the two families initially reacted."

"But it's probably safe to assume that Michael went a little nuts, especially after what we've both read in his e-mails."

"That's a safe assumption, however, no evidence supports that," Dunn said. "Those e-mails you've been receiving are just words."

"Words or not, he's a dangerous man. Terrorists don't have to blow something up before they're arrested."

"I see your point, Ms. Burkoff. The Knutson's don't see Michael as a threat though. These are two incredibly different scenarios."

"So that's it then? The Knutson's aren't concerned about Michael in the least bit and Michael gave you the look of innocence when you went to see him. I don't buy it. I'm not looking to say 'I told you so' at the end of this, but if someone doesn't do something soon to stop Michael, and maybe his son for that matter, I'm afraid someone is going to end up dead and it could be any number of people at this point."

"I'll still keep an eye on Michael. It's illegal for him to be on their property at night peeking in their windows. That son worries me too. I can take a trip over to the high school to see if I can learn anything else about his behaviors of late."

"That's a start. I wish you could do more," I said, feeling more helpless by the minute. Remembering the other reason I called to speak with him, I asked, "Did you happen to notice what type of vehicle Michael drove? You never got back to me on that like you promised."

"My apologies," he said, sighing. "He drives a tan Honda CR-V."

"Okay." It was definitely not an SUV in my driveway the other night.

I thanked the investigator for his time.

Something more needed to be done. Someone needed to watch Michael at all times. He couldn't be trusted. His compulsion to kill was getting stronger. And what about Mr. Knutson's reaction? How was he protecting his family? Was that really him smoking a cigarette in his front yard while the Calhoun men scampered off into the night? Maybe it was time for me to pay the Knutson's a visit. Maybe Investigator Dunn didn't paint the full picture for them. Maybe it was up to me to save this family.

30

"I'm running late," Kendall called to say when the clock ticked past ten o'clock. We were heading back to our hometown for the weekend to attend a high school classmate's wedding and she volunteered to drive. Fortunately, we didn't have to ride in the minivan because Jason needed it while he stayed home with the kids. We were going to drive in style in his Mustang. The car was already ten years old and it was all he had from his days before having kids, so he was very protective of it and only let Kendall drive it on special occasions.

"Well, hurry up. I promised my dad you would drop me off at his office in time for us to go to lunch."

"I just have to wait for a load of laundry to finish up. I'll be there in a half hour."

A half hour, huh? How could I kill the time? I knew what I wasn't going to do. I wasn't going to check my e-mail and ruin my fun-filled weekend. I didn't care if Michael and Gabe went off the deep end and took out the entire Knutson family. Okay, so I did care. I had Investigator Dunn's phone number in my phone and he knew how to reach me. I had to cross my fingers that nothing drastic happened while I was away, even though I had absolutely no control over any of it.

Not wanting to get involved with anything important, I slunk down into the couch to watch the rest of *The Price is Right*. It wasn't quite like the days with Bob Barker, but it would do. Just as the first spin of the wheel was about to start, Kevin called. I considered letting it go to voicemail.

"I wanted to say good-bye and to tell you to have a good time. Although, I don't doubt that you and Kendall always have a good time when you go back home together."

"Thanks. I am looking forward to it. Kendall is *really* looking forward to it. She hasn't had a weekend without the kids in almost a year."

"She might've mentioned that about ten times when I saw her earlier this morning."

"She was at work?"

"Yeah, she said she had one last item to finish before she felt right about taking the day off."

"One day away from the office. I can only imagine what it's like at home. She's probably been giving Jason orders all morning. He'll be just as happy to see her leave."

Our laughter soon turned to silence. There was something on Kevin's mind that he was hesitating to bring up. Knowing him it probably had to do with our relationship status. To avoid the topic I filled the conversation gap by telling him about the latest e-mail from Gabe and what Investigator Dunn and I had discussed on the phone.

"It's hard to believe the Knutson's aren't bothered by what they heard about Michael," Kevin said. "If that were me, I'd get a restraining order or put up an electric fence."

"I agree. Something just doesn't add up." Kendall pulled into the driveway. "Kevin, my chariot awaits. I'll give you a call when I get home on Sunday."

"Sure," he said.

Still sensing there was more to his phone call, I blatantly asked, "What is it, Kevin? What's bothering you?"

"Nothing, Kody. Have a great weekend. We can talk when you get back."

There was nothing worse than having someone tell you nothing was wrong when clearly something wasn't quite right. He didn't just call to say good-bye or to tell me to have fun this weekend. And he didn't call to ask me out. He wanted to talk about us. Ugh! Could anything be worse than trying to put a label on our relationship? I didn't know what to tell him. And I certainly didn't want him to profess his love for me if I wasn't ready to reciprocate. Poor guy! He was a saint for putting up with me. I had been giving him a lot of mixed signals lately. Maybe he would just agree to be friends with benefits. Lots of people did that these days. Was I too old for that sort of behavior?

"Did you bring your dancing shoes?" Kendall asked when I sat down in the Mustang. She had a huge smile on her face. This mom was off duty.

"I'm ready to get my groove on if that's what you mean," I said, playing along.

"Good to hear because I'm ready to party. I feel so free I don't know what to do first."

"Well, first let's leave my driveway and then we can make plans for the rest of the weekend."

Kendall threw in a CD with all our favorite songs from high school. We listened to a song by our favorite boy band, 98 Degrees, while we set up a game plan for the day. The ceremony was at four o'clock so that didn't give us a lot of time to play with. Even so, Kendall was hell bent on making every second count. She even made me feel like I had some newfound freedom even though I lived a life without many restrictions. Her energy was contagious.

The old music also got us reminiscing. I couldn't help but feel the guilty devastation all over again when she brought up Bloody Mary. Mary was a girl in our class who got her period in the seventh grade.

155

This was evident from the red stains between her legs that showed brightly on the white pants she wore. No one ever forgot that day, including Mary. That nickname remained with her all through high school. I even referred to her by that name. I, too, was a cruel human being.

During a song I didn't particularly care for, I turned the volume down to confess my fear of seeing Paul at the wedding.

"Don't stress it, Kody. Let the past go. I'm sure he's doing the same thing. The poor guy's just been through a divorce. If he is there, he'll be looking to have a good time."

"Yeah, you're probably right."

"Can you repeat that?"

My dirty look was answer enough. I hated when she did that.

Since our hometown was only fifty miles away, it didn't take us long to reach our destination. We drove slowly past our high school that was located on the edge of town. A new outdoor swimming pool had been added on since Kendall and I attended school there. The pool was overflowing with children of all ages. From the road we could see the little ones splashing in the water and going down the small slide. The older kids were huddled in groups along the edge. I had to remind Kendall to keep her eyes on the road.

"I hope the kids are doing okay," she said.

"I'm sure they're fine," I said, knowing full well that Jason had everything under control. He and the kids were going to have a great weekend. They, too, were going to feel a little bit of freedom.

Stopping outside my dad's office, we agreed to meet at the church shortly before the ceremony started. Both of our parents had also received invitations so we would be arriving separately with them. This separation allowed me to have a hearty lunch with my dad who I knew loved going out to eat without my mom. My mom was always on his case about the food choices he made. I think that was the case with a lot of older married couples. The wife felt the need to continue caring for someone after the kids were gone so the husband received that caring whether he wanted it or not. Therefore, my dad was always really happy to see my brother and me.

Our conversation was all over the place. We both liked to keep it fairly simple. He'd rather not hear about my clients' lives and I'd rather not hear about the newest vehicles on his lot, which left us talking about vacations we wanted to take someday. It was a welcome reprieve. My job was discussing the past, my friends and I were obsessed with the here and now, but when did I ever get to sink into the maybe someday? Not very often, that's when. I heard a lot of the same details about the cruise that my mom had told me when we met for lunch. He took it one step further though and outlined the next cruise he had lined up. He had grand plans for him and my mom. It was really sweet to hear.

Back at the house, the three of us went our separate ways to get all gussied up for the big event. Kendall had helped me pick out my dress, which I must say looked rather smashing on me. It was flowery, flowy, and showed off all the hard work I did over the winter working out at the gym. I even changed my earrings, which I rarely did, and sported a shoe with a bit of a heel. Exciting, I know.

The church was buzzing with guests when we arrived. It was a beautiful day so most of the people were congregating out in the parking lot. I immediately saw Kendall. I really couldn't miss her. She was wearing a bright orange dress with fuchsia sandals. I told her she looked like a traffic cone, but she only shrugged me off with that look that said I knew nothing about fashion.

The wedding was a standard Lutheran wedding. Not too long, not too short. The bridal party couldn't get out of the church fast enough. A white Hummer limousine waited out front to take them away to celebrate in private, well, as private as the bar scene was in town, before arriving at the reception.

As the rest of the rows filed out before us, I saw the familiar face from only a week ago. Paul looked devastatingly handsome as he walked down the aisle, his mother's arm linked with his while his father trailed close behind. Fortunately, he was looking straight ahead and I was out of his peripheral vision. Even though I was out of his line of sight, he remained in mine. My eyes followed him while that all too familiar nervous energy filled my belly. Did this feeling mean I was ready to let go of my anger? Was I ready to leave those two irresponsible teenagers in the past? As I rubbed my sweaty palms on my dress, I thought maybe. Maybe it was time.

"She looked stunning," my mother gushed as my dad drove us to the reception. "Kody, did you get a picture of her dress because I think that cut would look really good on you."

"It was nice," I said, still thinking about Paul.

"They look like such a nice couple. I only hope she slims down before they have children. That extra weight she's carrying around might cause some problems, not only with her pregnancy, but with their marriage too."

"Mother! Lynn!" my dad and I shouted in unison.

"What? I'm only saying what you all were thinking. Honesty is the best policy, you know."

"Not always," I said, rolling my eyes.

I quickly exited the car when we pulled up to the community center where the reception was being held. I didn't want any of my mom's honesty aimed at me, although I was sure she would honestly point out all the potential bachelors in town before the night was over. I hadn't told her about Kevin and me yet. I mean, there was nothing to tell. We weren't officially back together since I dodged that conversation this morning. As of right now I was still single. Woo hoo. Yippee. Boo. Hiss.

The evening rolled on without a hitch. I laughed with old friends, spent a good amount of time on the dance floor, and even took a couple of shots with Kendall since she was dead set on making the evening a night to remember, or forget, which was what I was banking on. My only disappointment was that Paul hadn't joined the festivities. Here I was set to forgive and forget and it was all for naught. I imagine he wasn't up for being social quite yet being that he was recently divorced. Even though he made it sound like it was his idea to end the marriage, he at one time had loved his wife with all his heart. I at least knew that about him. He let a person know that they were special.

Sitting down to take a rest and escape the drunkenness on the dance floor, I felt a tap on my shoulder. Assuming it was Kendall, I said, "I'm sitting this one out." Not hearing the smartass response I was expecting, I turned around.

"You're here," I said, fumbling to get my hair under control. The heat emanating from the dance floor had made for a curly, unmanageable mess even Vidal Sassoon couldn't tame. "I didn't think you were coming."

Smiling, Paul said, "You look great, Kody. You look like you've had a great time."

I stopped fussing with my hair. "Did you just get here?"

"Yeah. I contemplated coming all night. I just didn't want to answer a bunch of questions, you know? I figured by now everyone was probably drunk enough to leave me alone. Either that, or they'd be brave enough to be brutally honest." Giving me a questioning look, he continued. "You're not going to be brutally honest are you?"

"No," I said as sober as possible. Now that he was here I didn't want to scare him away. "I've had plenty to drink, mind you, but I'm still in fairly good shape. That's more than I can say for about half the people here, including Kendall. I'll be dragging her out of here."

An awkward silence followed our laughter.

"Nice wedding, huh?" I said, filling the void.

He grabbed a chair and placed it next to mine. He looked serious.

"Are we okay, Kody? You and me? When I went to see you at your office I didn't intend for it to be like that. I didn't know how it was going to be seeing you again. I only wanted to clear the air of a few things."

"Paul," I said, trying to interrupt. He held up his hand to signal that there was more he was prepared to say.

"I came to apologize that day, Kody. I had a whole speech planned, except only the first two lines came out. You didn't exactly help matters any with the way you were acting. I guess me showing up unannounced caught you off guard."

"It did," I agreed.

"Well, I came to say I was sorry. I'm sorry for how I handled everything back then. I'm sorry I didn't do more for you. I was scared out of my mind at the time. I had that scholarship and losing the opportunity to study at one of the best schools in the country was all I could think about. It was incredibly selfish of me so that's why I kept my mouth shut. It was wrong of me to do. I shouldn't have treated you that way.

"Having matured a little since high school, I know now that what happened between us couldn't have been easy for you. I left it up to you to make a huge decision, although I kind of got the impression that you wanted me out of the picture. You were so angry with me. Looking back, I realize that being alone wasn't what you wanted at all. You just didn't know how to ask for help and I didn't know how to give it, or I wasn't willing to give it. We were two confused kids who created something very grown-up." He took my hand and looked deep into my eyes. "I left you alone when you really needed me. You needed a friend. Friends don't do that to each other, especially when I loved you like I did."

I didn't respond. I couldn't respond. What he had just said was what I needed to hear from him. I followed his gaze out to the dance floor. There were only a few couples left dancing to a slow song being played by the deejay. The remainder of the guests were scattered about the room. The bride and groom had long since gone.

"Do you want to dance?" Paul asked, his hand still holding mine.

I looked at him again, trying to see the man in front of me instead of the boy I once knew so well. This was the perfect opportunity to tell him that he was right about me needing him. I did need him. I could have used a friend, a friend that knew what I was suffering through. It was also the right time to accept his apology. It was the right time, yet it wasn't only him that needed to apologize. Even though I needed him when the test showed positive, I wanted to be alone. I wanted to handle it by myself. I didn't want to hear what he had to say. If anything, I was the one who should apologize.

"Yes," I said.

Paul led me to the dance floor. We held on to each other as if doing so made all the wrongs right. This was what I had wanted that summer. This was what my heart yearned for, but my mind forbade.

31

"I still don't feel quite right. Yesterday was bad enough, but a two-day hangover? That's ridiculous," Kendall said with her hands over her stomach.

"You had quite a bit to drink at the reception. I didn't have the heart to tell you to stop."

"I know. I'm getting too old to party like that. It'll be at least a year before I do that again."

"That soon?" I teased.

"You're not making me feel any better."

"Sorry."

Kendall leaned against the inside of the car door. Because she still wasn't feeling one hundred percent, I offered to drive. I also got her to agree to stop in Bergan where the Knutson's and Calhoun's lived. It was completely out of the way, but as long as I drove, bought her lunch, and filled her in on what was going on with Michael, she was a willing participant. Plus, she wasn't ready for her "freedom weekend" to be over yet.

"Paul?" she asked.

"What about him?" I replied, fairly certain that she hadn't seen us on the dance floor. I also wasn't about to give away more information than I had to.

"Did he ever show up? Did you talk to him?"

Whoa. She must have drunk more than I gave her credit for. I swear I saw her give him a hug on his way out the door.

"Yeah, we talked for a little bit. It was nice. Like you said, the past is the past and we've all lived a lot of life since high school."

It *was* nice seeing him. It was especially nice not to be angry anymore. The reality of the matter was that we both made mistakes. We were both confused, scared, and then selfishly relieved by the outcome. Our relationship never would have lasted anyway after he left for college. I only knew of one couple from high school that was now married. The odds were against us from the start, but from where we left things last night, I wondered if the odds were once again in our favor.

"Apparently I haven't lived enough because I still feel like I'm in high school," she said, talking about her hangover.

Guilty of being happy that Kendall was wallowing in self-pity and uninterested in my interactions with Paul, I suggested she try to rest for the remainder of the drive. It was beneficial to both of us because I needed the quiet time to figure out exactly what it was I planned to do in Bergan. I knew I needed to visit the Knutson's to convince them that Michael was a real threat to their family. I didn't know, however, how I was going to introduce myself. I couldn't exactly tell them the truth.

* * * *

"Hi! I hope I'm not interrupting anything," I said, reaching out to shake Mr. Knutson's hand. He was a tall man, large in stature, muscular. His short, dark hair and graying goatee put him in his early forties. He didn't appear happy to see me at his door.

"What are you selling?" he asked gruffly.

"I'm here visiting neighbors like you on behalf of a consulting neighborhood watch group hired by the City of Bergan. If it's okay, I'd like to ask you a few questions about the safety of your neighborhood." Before he had time to tell me he wasn't interested, I asked the first question. "Do you feel generally safe in your neighborhood?"

"Yes, I do," he answered immediately.

"Good to hear," I said, making a checkmark in the notebook I found in the back seat of Jason's car. My act had to be believable. "Do you worry about theft when you're away from your home?"

"No."

"Have you seen any suspicious activity within the last few weeks?"

"What do you mean exactly?" he asked.

I held my response. We were about to have company.

"Peder," he said, turning to his son, "this nice lady is checking into the safety of our neighborhood. She wants to know if we feel safe in our own home. Doesn't it make you feel good knowing that the City of Bergan is looking out for it's citizens?"

Peder raised his eyebrows and shifted his eyes between his father and me. He looked just like the photo I found in the newspaper. He was quite a bit shorter than his dad, but the resemblance was there. The distrust I felt from his father would come with time.

"That's nice to know," he said, followed by, "Mom says lunch is ready."

"Tell her I'll be right there. I don't doubt that this interview is about over."

As Peder left me and his father to continue, I sucked in a big breath of air willing myself not to turn around and make a run for it.

"Now where were we?" Mr. Knutson asked, straightening his back and lowering his chin. He was trying to intimidate me.

Holding my ground, I said, "I was asking about suspicious activity. Unfamiliar cars parked in the road? Strangers roaming the streets late at night? Maybe even a peeping tom?"

His eyes widened and he took a small step back. I had obviously hit on something.

"I haven't seen any of that around here," he said, looking past me. "I get a sound night's sleep without any disturbances most nights. Occasionally, I'll hear a dog barking, but that doesn't last long. I'm certain you'll get the same response from everyone around here. This is a nice place to live."

"I don't doubt that, sir." Without pausing, I asked, "Do you have a security system, window sensors, or anything else you use for private protection?"

"No, I don't believe in that." He hitched up his jeans. "It's not any of your business, but I keep a registered .357 revolver in my nightstand."

"I thought you said you weren't worried about your family's safety?"

"I'm not."

"Then why the gun?" Oops. That comment wasn't supposed to leave my lips. I swear.

He leaned forward, placing a hand on my shoulder. "I will protect my family if and when I need to."

Point taken.

Shrinking away from his touch, I said, "Before I go, the City of Bergan wants to know if there is anything they can do to better serve your community."

Without hesitation, he said, "They can stop wasting taxpayer's money on people like you."

Backing down the steps, I thanked him for his time. I felt his glare bore into my back as I left his property.

My pace quickened once I turned the corner and saw the Mustang. Kendall's arms flew up around her head when I slammed the car door shut.

"Take it easy. My head feels like it's going to explode," she yelled.

"That man gave me the creeps. He's way scarier than either of our dads."

"Your dad is a salesman and mine is an optometrist."

"He's in denial or something," I said, ignoring her comment. "You can't tell me he doesn't know about Michael stalking his son day and night. It doesn't make sense. Why is he afraid to ask for help?"

"He's a man. Men don't ask for help unless they're dying or there's no toilet paper in the bathroom," Kendall said from her huddled position.

"This is no time for jokes. Someone is trying to kill his son and he acts like he isn't in the least bit worried."

"Maybe he truly doesn't know his son is in any danger."

"Or maybe he has a plan to take care of Michael on his own. If that were the case though, wouldn't he have done something already? He had the perfect opportunity the other night. Michael's son said he saw someone outside smoking a cigarette when he and his dad were leaving the area. I smelled smoke on Mr. Knutson just now."

"Plenty of people smoke," Kendall added.

"He told me he has a gun in his nightstand."

"Who doesn't these days?"

Wanting Kendall to shut up and go back to her catatonic state, I let the subject die. I wasn't going to convince her of anything, nor did I need to. I knew something wasn't quite right with the situation and that's all that mattered.

A few hours later I dropped myself off at home and told Kendall that I hoped she felt better in the morning. There was no way her hangover would last three days, right? Once inside I gave my cat, Percy, some love and then started unpacking. I typically left the suitcase on my bedroom floor for at least a week after a trip, but with only a few pairs of underwear left in my drawer throwing in a load of laundry was mandatory. Those remaining undies were only worn for special occasions, if you know what I mean.

As if he knew I was rifling through my undergarments, I received a text message from Kevin. "Lunch tomorrow?" it read. Hmm. Sounded harmless enough, but I knew what he wanted to discuss. He wanted to know if we were boyfriend and girlfriend again. How long could I prolong the inevitable? He didn't like being in limbo any more than I did. I was making life uncomfortable for the both of us by avoiding the discussion. Figuring I'd have enough time between now and then to come up with a clever way to remain semi-single, I accepted his offer.

32

Why can't my dad tell the truth? Investigator Dunn asked him if he had seen Michael Calhoun and his creepy son sneaking around our house. Even that strange woman hired by the City was asking about peeping toms. Those were the perfect opportunities to ask for help. If only I had the guts to speak up. I promised him though. I promised to let him take care of things, whatever that meant.

Ever since the accident, everything has been so messed up. My parents were ultra protective any time I went out, and then if my mom had one of her anxiety attacks she would call me to come home or else her and my dad would show up at whatever game I was attending to make sure that I was okay. It wasn't normal. I guess it never will be normal until I get out of this god-forsaken town. I never wanted to move here to begin with and now my dad says we can't leave because that's what everyone wants us to do. Why not do what they want us to do? Maybe we can live normal lives again. Maybe I'll someday be able to go to sleep at night and not wonder if I'll wake up with a gun pointed at my head.

I see him sometimes. I know he's there. I can feel his stare. It's not just at home either. He follows me around town too. He'll be in the lobby of the movie theater when I walk out or in the summer he'll sit at a picnic table in the park where some friends and I shoot hoops. Gabe isn't much better. He's always lurking behind corners. I actually feel sorry for him. He can't help what he's turned into.

I don't know how many times I, or anyone else, can tell Michael Calhoun that Julia's death was an accident. I didn't push her. I didn't try to seduce her into my tent. I didn't even ask her to come with us. Her following us was all her doing. She was being really goofy, obviously trying to get our attention. Later, the guys claimed it was my attention she was after. I guess I sort of knew that. I couldn't figure it out though. There were plenty of guys in her grade, and that were there that day, that she could have dated.

She followed us back to our tent where we cracked a few beers, turned up the music, and messed around while we waited for the next concert to start. It didn't take long for the wrestling to begin. I learned that it was customary for the other guys to challenge the one wrestler in the bunch who was already a two-time state champion. A few guys took their turns and were pinned within seconds. From what I had seen, I knew I didn't have a chance either. He was so quick.

When it was finally my turn, instead of challenging him alone, I thought it would be funny to bring Julia into the match with me. I picked her up in my arms and we started spinning in circles toward the guy, trying to knock him down with her legs. She couldn't stop laughing. We were all having a good time watching the champ duck and dodge out of the way, yet still looking for a way to take my legs out from under me. It was all fun and games until I spun one too many times. What happened next has replayed in my mind more times than I can count. I lost my balance. We fell. Julia was knocked unconscious.

It happened so fast, yet every time it replayed in my mind it was in slow motion. One minute I heard her laughter, the next minute there was nothing but silence. Deathly silence. Julia didn't move. Her eyes were open and her cheeks were still flushed, but a growing pool of blood under her head signaled that something was wrong. Seriously wrong. I was frozen with fear. All I could do was sit down next to her and will her to get up with my eyes. My gaze eventually left her to seek help from the others. When I did, one of the guys rushed over to check her pulse. Another one ran off to get help. A few others got on their cell phones to call 911 or their parents.

Help was on its way, for whatever it was worth. Julia was dead. There wasn't anything anyone could do to bring her back to life. It was so instant, so final. How could I have been holding a living human being in my arms one minute and then the next minute the life was draining out the back of her head? The reality of the situation didn't take long to sink in. I knew at that moment my life was forever changed.

It's been almost a year since the night Julia died. We were all still dealing with it. The kids at school were probably the most forgiving. The ones who were at the campsite knew it was an accident and reported it back that way. The adults were the ones that continued to give me snide looks or looks that said, "You should be the one buried six feet deep." Some have even said harsh words directly to my face in front of my friends. I hated them. They weren't there. They didn't know what happened. All they knew was that the beautiful Julia Calhoun was gone from this world and I was the last one to have contact with her. I couldn't say it enough. It was an accident and I was truly sorry that it happened.

33

To: kodyburkoff@inyourwords.com
From: sad_dad1@gmail.com
Subject: Was it you?

Was it you who sent the police to my doorstep? Maybe you've figured out my identity. Maybe you know everything about me, the case, about Julia and her murderer. The press painted such a sympathetic picture of that boy. He played right along with it too. I heard from teachers that he suffered from depression this past school year. I don't know why they felt it necessary to tell me that. I don't care. I, too, suffered from depression. My whole family did. Hell, my doctors tell me I'm still suffering, but you already know that. I'm not telling you anything new.

It looks like you had a lot of fun at the wedding this weekend. Don't forget I know everything about you too.

sad dad

34

"Michael Calhoun was my friend on Facebook," I confessed to Kevin at our lunch date on Monday. We had only ordered our drinks before I blurted out the information. Of course, Facebook was the culprit. How could I have been so naïve? And now thanks to Michael's friendly reminder, I was even more paranoid than before. Was he threatening me? Do I deny going to the police or do I tell him I did it for his own good? Would he even understand?

"Call me a name. I deserve it," I said, ready to take a verbal punch. It hurt worse when someone else called me a name and I was more than ready to feel the pain. It was my own form of self-mutilation.

"Are you serious? You've been Facebook friends with this creep the entire time? How did you not know that?"

"I don't know. I'm friends," I said, using finger quotes, "with a lot of people. I don't always know them when I accept their request." Saying that made me feel like an even bigger idiot.

"I know everyone on my friend list," Kevin retorted.

"That's because you only have like twenty-three friends. How hard is that?"

"Idiot," Kevin said straight-faced.

"Thank you. What else you got?"

"Moron. Stupid. Dummy."

"Those are good."

"Imbecile. Dipshit."

"Okay. You can stop now," I said, holding both hands in the air as if to surrender.

"Are you sure? I can think of more."

Kevin seemed to be really enjoying himself. I actually felt better too.

"I know this is a dumb question and I shouldn't even have to ask," Kevin started, "but did you take him off your friend list?"

"Yes. I logged in right after I read the e-mail and scoured my friend list. It took hours. I should have taken the time to do it when Kendall mentioned the possibility."

Kevin shook his head.

"Don't say anything more. I feel dumb enough as it is."

"Regardless of how you feel, there's got to be more that can be done to stop this guy from harassing you and that poor family."

"I sort of already did something more," I said.

With his head cocked, he asked, "What exactly did you sort of do, Kody?"

"It wasn't anything illegal. I don't think so anyway," I answered. I filled Kevin in on the stunt I pulled yesterday at the Knutson's. "Don't you think it's odd that the family, or the father I should say, isn't worried or that he acts unaware of Michael still feeling such aggression toward his son?" I asked Kevin before he reprimanded me for my actions.

"It is a little hard to swallow, especially being that Michael's son saw someone standing outside the house when he was leaving."

"The father owns a gun too, which makes me wonder if he might be planning to do something on his own."

"Don't you think he would have done it by now if that was his plan? You said it's been almost a year. I would be willing to bet that Mr. Knutson has had plenty of opportunities."

"I completely agree with you. Even with my skepticism of Mr. Knutson, I can't get over the feeling of obligation I have toward protecting Peder. I've read Michael's worst thoughts. I know where he goes at night while the family is sleeping. I know that Gabe also blames Peder for the hardship in his childhood."

With neither of us having an immediate solution to the problem, we began to eat the meal the server set in front of us. Interrupting the sound of forks hitting our plates, Kevin asked the question I had been anticipating.

"Is this a good time to talk about us?"

No, I thought to myself. "What do you want to talk about?" I asked.

"Well, we never really discussed the other night."

"Sometimes actions speak louder than words."

"Sometimes words need to be spoken."

I pushed the food around on my plate. "Look, Kevin, what happened the other night was completely spontaneous."

"It was amazing."

I blushed.

"Because of what happened, does that mean we're getting back together? I don't know."

"Do you want to at least try?" Kevin asked.

"I don't know. What if it doesn't work again?"

"What if it does? What if I'm your prince charming?"

"Stop it."

"Seriously, I can rent a couple of white horses and a carriage if I need to. I'll even make sure the blinds in the carriage go down nice and smooth so you can ravage me again."

He certainly was pulling out all the stops this time.

"What makes you think I would want to ravage you again?"

"You're not going to let this get away from you," he said, motioning to himself.

"Those khakis are awfully enticing," I winked.

"I saw you checking me out when I got here."

I couldn't stop smiling. If Kevin and I got along this well all the time, we might stand a chance. He certainly was charming and adorable. But best of all, he genuinely liked me. I didn't have to be someone I wasn't when I was around him.

"Do we have to put a label on our relationship or can we just wing it?"

"We can do whatever you would like."

"I'd like to keep it spontaneous, for now at least."

"I'll always live in the now if you're in it."

"That was cheesy."

"I know."

* * * *

"You got a couple of minutes?" Charlie asked, peeking through the door only minutes after I returned from my lunch date with Kevin.

"Sure, Charlie. What's up?"

"Well, I know my memoir is basically done and I really shouldn't be bothering you, but you know more about me than most folks, especially when it comes to the women in my life. I guess I was hoping you could help me out with something personal."

"I think we can consider ourselves to be friends," I said.

Charlie had me curious. He was real fidgety, which wasn't like him, and he was having a hard time keeping eye contact. Something was definitely bothering him. He pulled out a chair and waited for me to join him before sitting down. Once we were both seated, the strange behavior continued.

"Is everything okay, Charlie? How is it with Catherine living with you again?"

"It's going great actually. She found a job at the thrift store. I don't know if she's pocketing things again, but she sure does seem happy. It's not like that stuff is worth anything."

When I was about to ask about his relationship with her, he blurted out, "She sleeps in the other bedroom. We haven't, you know, been intimate yet."

"Yet?" I asked, not wanting to know the answer, but I had a feeling that was why he was here.

"I'm giving her space. If and when she's ready to take that next step, I'll be ready too."

"What about that other woman you were seeing? Is she still in the picture?"

A huge smile spread across his face.

"You sly dog! You're juggling two women at once?" I said in disbelief.

"It's not quite like that, Kody. Catherine and I are playing house with no benefits. Azelia and I are only interested in the benefits. That woman is amazing, by the way. The things she can do in the..."

I held up my hand. "Not too many details, okay Charlie?"

"Sorry about that," he said, sitting back in his chair. "I've got it working pretty slick right now and neither of them really mind each other. Azelia was even over for dinner the other night. They got along fine and the food was great. Catherine has always been a great cook."

"So, what's the problem? It sounds like every man's dream. You have one woman tending to your every need in the kitchen, while the other one tends to your every need in the bedroom."

He drummed his fingers on the table and then mumbled something I couldn't quite understand.

"What was that? I couldn't hear you," I said.

"I'm thinking about asking them to have a threesome."

I blew back in my chair as if a jet were taking off right in front of me.

"Why are you telling me this? I can't help you with something like that."

"I just thought since you were young and playing the dating game you might know what to do in this situation."

"You thought I might know what to do about having a threesome?" I asked, over enunciating each word.

"It sounds worse when you say it like that," he grumbled.

Charlie's face was the color of a freshly painted fire hydrant. Mine was maybe one shade lighter.

"I can't believe you thought I could help you with something like this. What you do in your bedroom is your business."

"Geez, Kody, I know that. I was hoping for some pointers or something, or even a vote of confidence. I'm an old man trying to get laid by two women. It's a pretty big deal to me."

I started laughing uncontrollably and didn't allow myself to stop. Eventually my cheeks began to hurt from laughing so hard. Charlie, assumingly embarrassed and unable to admit what a foolish mistake he had made, let himself out. I must have looked ridiculous to anyone peering in from the outside; a woman all alone, doubled over with laughter. I hadn't laughed that hard in a long time. It felt really good, even if it was at the expense of someone else.

What did I ever say to give that man the impression I knew a thing or two about threesomes? I couldn't wait to share this with Kendall. Confidential or not, this was too good to keep all to myself.

35

To: sad_dad1@gmail.com
From: kodyburkoff@inyourwords.com
Subject: It's for your own good

I know who you are. I know where you live. I asked the police to keep an eye on you. It's for your own good.

Don't you see, Michael, you'll lose all you have left if you cause harm to Peder and his family? Do you even know how that will affect your son? He knows everything, Michael. He follows you at night. He watches you as you sit outside Peder's window holding a gun in your hands.

My intentions in telling you this aren't to get Gabe into trouble, but to tell you the kind of example you are being to your son. I know your relationship with him is rocky at best, but Gabe looks up to you. He supports you. He will do anything for you, including commit murder. Check your Sent folder. Read what he's written to me. See for yourself how your words and actions are affecting him. I think you'll be surprised.

Stop your compulsion to kill before it's too late. Get help, Michael. If you don't do it for yourself, then do it for your son.

Kody

36

Doing all I could to stay focused on one thing, I tried working on some magazine articles I had started but never finished. I didn't even know why I was attempting to write them being that they were about using your time effectively. Staring at the screen thinking about ten different things at once was hardly an effective use of my time. Perhaps some mileage on the treadmill was what I needed. Perhaps it wasn't. I half-heartedly grabbed my gym bag and locked the front door behind me.

With my eyes locked on an infomercial and having the entire gym virtually to myself, I got into a groove and was already feeling better. The hot instructor even winked at me on his way out of the locker room. That was his token greeting to all the women, but it gave me goosebumps all the same.

After a fierce workout, which was about a half hour of running, I headed back into the locker room feeling sweaty and accomplished. Seated on a small stool just outside the entrance was a boy folding towels. He looked vaguely familiar. I walked past him slow enough so that my brain had time to register his face. Then it hit me. He was the boy who came into my office talking nonsense about some zombie apocalypse. How could I forget him or our conversation?

"You're Alex, right?" I asked.

He nodded as he continued to manipulate the bleached cotton.

"You came into my office not too long ago trying to convince me of a zombie apocalypse."

He looked from side to side while shushing me with his finger. "Don't say that around here. My mom might hear you."

"Your mom?" I whispered.

"Yeah, she owns the place. If she hears any more zombie talk, I'll be cleaning toilets instead of folding these towels."

I tried not laugh. I found the whole idea rather humorous. A mom grounding her son to towel duty at the gym because he believed zombies were going to invade our land and kill every last one of us.

It was obvious that Alex didn't want to engage in any more conversation that might further his troubles at home so I made my way to the showers. As I left the building, I waved at his buff mother standing behind the counter. I immediately saw the resemblance. Outside the building, my lips formed a snarl. I hated when women looked better than I did and they had already given birth. I thought it was only fair that married women with children pack on a few pounds to make us single ladies stand out a little more. It wasn't too much to ask.

Dropping my gym bag off in my car before going back into the office, I noticed that Sam had parked his car next to mine. It wasn't until I saw the driver's side door open that I realized he was still in it. His head must not reach above the head rest. Easy mistake, I suppose.

"Howdy, neighbor," he said.

I was thankful he at least understood our relationship.

"Hi, Sam," I said on my way to the back door. My reaction was definitely less hostile than the last time.

"You're not always going to be this way around me, are you?"

"What way is that exactly?" I asked with only a hint of attitude. Of course I knew what he was talking about. I thought it might be fun to hear how he described my behavior.

"Distant."

One word. That's it? He's not being much fun at all.

"We're neighbors," I said. "We can talk about the weather if you want, although there's not much to say with all this beautiful sunshine. There, I just started a conversation. Care to join in?"

His stunned expression said more than his words. "No thanks," he said before turning his back on me.

Wow! What a bitch! I didn't know I had it in me. I almost felt bad for being so mean, but then I rubbed my hands down my hips and felt rather justified. It also felt good knowing that I had almost completed an item on my bucket list: make an enemy. I know that sounds crazy. I shouldn't be trying to make enemies. Most enemies came naturally. Rocky Balboa was a natural enemy to that freakishly large Russian boxer. Then there was Batman and the Joker, Boss Hog and the Duke boys, and the Roadrunner and Wile E. Coyote. It just wasn't in my personality to have a natural enemy. You've heard of "Minnesota nice," right? We try to look for the positive in everyone, regardless of their demeanor. This was different. Sam gave me a reason to hate him, which made him the chosen one.

Adding to my rather odd day was the sight of Mrs. Lopez standing outside the front door. It wasn't odd that she was waiting for me because she's told me before that she knew I didn't travel too far. Apparently I was just that predictable. It was odd that she wore a large flowery hat. It wasn't your regular sunhat that you picked up from any big box store. It had real flowers on it and from a distance I thought I saw a piece of fruit. I couldn't wait to hear this story.

"Good afternoon. You look...um...summery," was all that sputtered out of my mouth. My stammering didn't even phase the delighted expression on her face.

"It's a gift from Emil. He had it made especially for me. He knows how much I like fresh flowers," she said, beaming from ear to ear.

"That was considerate of him," I said even though I thought the hat looked ridiculous. "You're still seeing Emil, huh? It must be getting serious."

"Oh, Kody, we're just having a good time together. That's about as serious as I'll ever get. He makes me smile and that's what's important."

"You're right. A man that can make you smile is a keeper. It's also beneficial if he can cook, clean, and get the kids to bed. Those are Kendall's words, not mine."

"Kendall is a smart woman."

"That's what she says too."

After we both enjoyed some humor at my best friend's expense, we settled ourselves down into our usual seats.

"So what brings you here this fine July day?" I asked.

"You might think this is strange, Kody, because I know I do. I was eating my oatmeal this morning, like I do just about every morning, and in the bowl I saw what looked like the profile of my mother."

Was she serious? Wearing that hat and now seeing images in her oatmeal?

"My mother died many years ago so when I saw her image this morning I couldn't help but think that she was watching over me today. Today's my birthday. You probably didn't know that."

"No, I didn't. Happy birthday, Mrs. Lopez! That explains the unique gift from Emil. Is there a big celebration planned?"

"Yes, we're all gathering at my granddaughter's house. We're having an early dinner party because they think I can't stay awake past six o'clock. Ha! I'll have them know I occasionally stay up to watch Jay Leno. I don't share that with them though. They would make such a fuss."

Mrs. Lopez was such a spirited woman. I hoped that I had a quarter of her spunk when I reached her age.

"Well, I hope you have a great time. Will Emil be joining you?"

"I invited him. He didn't give me an answer either way. I've discovered that he can be quite mysterious at times, which I'm a bit fond of actually. I don't like the transparency of some of the old geezers I'm friends with. What you see is what you get with them.

With Emil, I have to be on my toes. I never quite know what he's up to."

"It is more fun that way, isn't it?" I said, thinking of my own experiences. It was fun to be spontaneous and to keep your partner guessing. Being able to finish one's sentences wasn't always a great attribute to have in a relationship. Too much predictability can lead to boredom, which can then lead to failure. No one wants to be bored, especially not me. That's one of the reasons why I was hesitant to get back together with Kevin. I know what he's going to say before he says it. I know how he'll react when I suggest we eat something other than pizza on a Friday night. I know that before he tries to make out with me he'll pause our movie to brush his teeth. It's sweet and all, but extremely predictable.

"It is," Mrs. Lopez agreed, her eyes glimmering in the sunlight. As soon as she came out of her trance-like state, she retraced her thoughts to the real reason why she stopped by to see me. "Her image, the one in the oatmeal, reminded me of how she used to try to teach me to draw. My mother was a great artist. Her specialty was portrait drawing. Everyone who came to our house knew it too because of all the drawings hung on our walls. I didn't even know who half the people were. Some of them were family I imagine, but I would bet some of them were complete strangers. Like me, my mother had a sense of adventure. So much so that she invited strangers to our house just so she could draw them. You can't do that these days. You never know who you might be inviting into your house."

"You certainly do have to be more careful," I added.

"It was obvious from the start that I hadn't inherited her artistic ability. That didn't bother her too much. She was more excited that one of her children showed some interest in drawing."

Mrs. Lopez went on to tell me about the different objects she and her mother drew when they found the time. I was only half listening because her story reminded me of when my mom and I spent some quality time together sewing. Like Mrs. Lopez, I hadn't inherited any special skills for the craft. I bobbled along acting like I enjoyed it when in reality I thought it was a waste of time because I could buy a much cuter shirt at the store without sticking my thumb with a needle fifty gazillion times. Sharing this wealth of knowledge was important to my mom so I rarely complained. However, even though I received this knowledge, I made a pledge to delete the information from memory when someone else felt it necessary to shove my brain full of craftiness. We all know our strengths and weaknesses. A crafter I was not.

"Do you still have some of your drawings or even some of your mother's?" I asked.

"Oh, I have a couple of her portraits up in my attic. I suppose some of mine are up there as well. I haven't looked at them in years, probably decades." She took off her hat and placed it on the table. I was able to get a closer look at the masterpiece. I was wrong about the fruit. It was a large orange flower that threw me off.

Mrs. Lopez continued. "Some things are better left in the past. Looking at them now would only make me miss her more. You never stop missing someone when they're gone. The hurt fades, but it never completely goes away."

"So I've heard," I said, unable to commiserate. I hadn't yet experienced the death of someone close to me. For that, I felt lucky.

"I better get to my party. Those great-grandchildren don't like to wait. They're even more spoiled than my grandchildren were."

"I don't doubt that. Have a wonderful birthday and tell Emil he did a great job picking out your gift," I said, giving her a hug.

"It is rather fabulous."

With Mrs. Lopez on her way to her party, I sat down at my desk to reflect on what had turned out to be one of the weirdest days on record. For starters, I ran into Alex, the zombie boy, at my gym. I solidified the notion of making Sam an enemy, natural or otherwise. Last, but not least, I listened to Mrs. Lopez tell me about the image of her mother she saw in her breakfast. Was I getting payback for something I did or said? Kendall and I were pretty catty on the drive to and from Wilcox, but this was ridiculous. The only thing that might top off the madness was another e-mail from Michael or Gabe. With a few clicks of the mouse, I learned that using the term madness wasn't too far off and at least one part of my day was predictable.

To: kodyburkoff@inyourwords.com
From: sad_dad1@gmail.com
Subject: Leave us alone

My dad's upset. I read your last e-mail. You know who we are, huh? I guess that's why the school counselor sent me a note asking me to meet her in her office during my study hall period today. Without giving me a reason, she asked all sorts of questions about my parents. How was it now that they were divorced? How were we all coping with Julia being gone? How did I feel about life in general? I lied and told her everything was fine. I wasn't about to tell her the truth. Being a counselor, I assume she saw right through me, but you never know. She didn't exactly look like she enjoyed her job.

Have you talked to the Knutson's? Did you tell them what my dad and I said in our e-mails? Do they know about our visits to their house? What am I thinking? Of course you did, even though your conversations with my dad are supposed to be confidential. You must be one of those goody two shoes who does no wrong even if it means getting sweet revenge. I can't believe that you're siding with my sister's murderer. You've read what Julia's death has done to our family. You know how messed up we all are. He's the one to blame. It's Peder's fault. You can't blame my dad for wanting to give that family exactly what they deserve. They deserve to feel the same emptiness we feel, the same sadness that never goes away day after day. I hate feeling this way. I want to be happy like everyone else. I can't help but wonder that if my dad does what I think he'll do one of these days, we all might feel a little better. It's worth a shot.

Stay away. Leave us alone. I'll look after my dad. He'll make the right decision. If not, I might work up the courage to do it for him. After all, he's my dad. Family needs to stick together.

37

"There's nothing I can do," Investigator Dunn said the next morning when I called. I wasn't as eager to go running to him after receiving Gabe's e-mail yesterday since he didn't exactly run off to fix things. "I can't ask for an officer to stake out the Knutson house when the family doesn't share the same fears as you do for your client."

"Ex-client," I added for clarity, which was more for me than him.

"Fine. Ex-client."

"What about *my* fears? Michael threatened me in his last e-mail. Gabe doesn't exactly sound any saner. The last thing I need is another psychopath hunting me down. Been there, done that."

"You can fill out a restraining order. Just go down to your…"

"That won't do me any good and you know it."

"What is it, Ms. Burkoff, that will make you happy and leave me alone so that I can do my job?" Dunn asked. It was obvious he was losing his patience with me.

"I want you to monitor Michael's every move."

"Not gonna happen."

"How about just during the night?"

"I don't think so."

"Come on, Dunn. You know it won't look good if something happens to the Knutson kid when you had prior knowledge of a potential threat."

"The family doesn't want help. End of story. Plus, I've known Michael for years and he would never hurt anyone. He's all talk. Always has been."

"People change. I've seen it firsthand. Losing someone you love can make you to do horrible, unthinkable things."

Dunn sighed heavily. "Here's what I'll do. I'll ask the night-shift officers to drive past Michael's place and the Knutson's for the next few nights. And that's only if they aren't busy with other calls."

"A lot of crime happening in Bergan, Minnesota?" I asked.

"Take it or leave it, Ms. Burkoff."

Dunn wasn't finding humor in my sarcasm. "I'll take it," I said before quickly ending the call. I didn't want to take any chances of saying something that might change his mind.

Even though I felt like I had won the battle with the investigator by having officers patrol the families' homes at night, I wondered if it was enough. Would police presence deter Michael from his habitual urges? Would Mr. Knutson tell them to go protect someone else if he noticed their repeat visits? Unfortunately, I wasn't convinced that police drive-bys were an effective solution to this out-of-the-ordinary problem. I wished there was something more I could do. The obvious solution, of course, was to take matters into my own hands and stake out the Knutson's home myself. One drawback was that they lived two hundred miles away. It wasn't as though I could take a casual drive over there to check on things during the night. Another problem was that I didn't know if Michael was a peeping tom on a daily basis. I hadn't yet determined if there was a pattern to his madness. That's when it hit me. I knew one night that he'd surely pay the Knutson's a visit: the anniversary of Julia's death.

Scrambling to locate the copy of Julia's obituary that I found in the archives of the Bergan weekly newspaper, I saw that the anniversary of Julia's death was sooner than I had hoped or remembered. It was tomorrow. There was no way Michael would miss out on this opportunity to remind Peder of how much he missed his daughter. I didn't know how he would do it exactly, but I was sure something was going to happen. Two other people were aware of tomorrow's date as well: Julia's mother and brother. I would be willing to bet that Gabe was thinking well ahead by making plans to stay with his dad tomorrow night, wanting to be around for the action. He made it painfully clear that he was his father's number one cheerleader.

Now that I was confident with the *who*, *when*, and *where*, I contemplated the *what* and *how*. How was I going to help either of the families? Was I going to barge into Michael's home demanding that he hand over the gun he kept in his car? Or was I going to go to the Knutson's and beg them to leave their home for this one night? Neither plan seemed logical or like a long-term solution, but then again none of the events leading up to this have been very sensible. Matters of the heart tended to be complicated.

The next big decision was whether to bother sharing this information with Investigator Dunn. Surely he would have mentioned the significance of tomorrow's date if he had picked up on it. But then again, he seemed to be doing as little as possible with this case and didn't even believe that Michael was capable of hurting someone. So when it came right down to it, I was the only one besides Gabe that thought Michael was capable of committing murder. I might be fighting this battle alone. Well, not entirely on my own. I needed a partner in crime, a real smooth operator. Since I didn't know any of those, I chose Kevin. He rarely told me no and I had something that he wanted. Me.

* * * *

"So, how about it? Are you coming with me or do I have to go alone?" I asked Kevin.

"You're crazy, you know that?"

"I know," I agreed. "I'll be even crazier if something bad happens tomorrow night and I'm not there to stop it."

"Why don't you call the police? They're the ones that get paid to do this."

"Investigator Dunn is doing all he can," I lied. "Police will be patrolling the area. I'm concerned that they'll miss something. If we're there, not a moment will go by without surveillance. We can call the police if and when we need to."

"I don't know, Kody. This sounds dangerous."

"I'm not asking you to risk your life, Kevin. I'm only asking you to sit in a parked car outside of someone's house with me. It might even be fun. We'll buy a bunch of junk food and have a good ol' time in your car."

"My car? Why's it got to be my car?"

"Michael might recognize mine from photos on Facebook."

"I'm feeling used."

"I thought you liked being used," I said as seductively as possible. "Remember when you came over to ease away my nightmares?"

"Yeah, I like being used that way," Kevin said. I assumed he had a smile on his face. Anytime a woman alluded to sex, a man's mind went slack, opening the door for further manipulation. I saw the crack in the opening and was fully prepared to bust the door down.

"You. Me. The back seat. Huh? What do you say?"

"I say I know when I'm being played. You would never do anything in the back seat of a car. We've dated before, remember?"

"Come on, Kevin. Just say you'll do it. It's only for one night," I begged. It was usually beneath me to beg, but I really didn't want to go to Bergan alone.

Silence filled the air.

Unsure of which way his decision was leaning, I continued to grovel. "You don't want me to go all by myself, do you?"

"Okay, I'll do it. Just stop sounding so pathetic."

"It works, doesn't it?" I said smugly.

"Whatever, Kody." He was obviously annoyed with himself for giving in to me. "What time do I need to pick you up?"

"After work is fine. You're the best, Kevin."

"I want to be."

Ignoring his last comment, I said, "I'll see you tomorrow night."

With Kevin's solemn final words and the reality of what I had planned for us, these next few days were going to be the longest of my life. At least Mary was coming in this morning. That guaranteed me concentrating on her life instead of my own, especially since her life was virtually in shambles. Realistically speaking, she was in a loveless marriage that left her with zero self-esteem.

It's amazing how others can affect one's self-esteem. Through words or expressions, people cast their approval or disapproval, and if you aren't secure enough in who you are, the negativity can take you right out of the game. It can trample you and shove you under the bed like that ugly sweater you wore only once to make your grandmother happy. If Mary asked for my opinion, I would tell her to shove her husband under the bed followed by some planks of wood and a box of nails. The stepdaughter had potential to see her evil ways as wrong. Most adults were rotten teenagers that grew into behaving citizens. Notice I said most. I knew at least a handful of adults that were still rotten to the core.

Speaking of rotten, there went Sam. He must have a hot date with a mannequin, a child-size one. Okay, so even I had a little bit of rotten still in me. I chose Sam as my enemy, remember? That's what enemies did, talked a lot of smack and toiled over their demise.

Interrupting the image I had conjured up of Sam and his date was the sight of Mary with a smile as bright as the sun. Yep, she was smiling and she looked super chic to boot. Double bonus. I don't say that about a lot of people because most of the people I hang out with are not chic. Nancy was the exception, of course. Kendall tried to dress like a cool mom, or so she said, but she didn't wear anything you couldn't pick up at Target. I gave her credit for trying.

"You look absolutely stunning," I said. "What's the occasion?"

"No occasion really. I'm meeting Nancy for lunch. She said she would meet me here after we were done. Didn't she tell you?"

"This is the first I'm hearing of it."

"Oh, well, she must have forgotten. Anyway, I'm ready to get started when you are."

"Right," I said, surprised. "Go ahead and have a seat."

I wanted to be more prepared for Mary's visit, but I honestly didn't know where to start. I didn't know if we had ever started. She wasn't a typical client in that we could pick up on a certain year or period during her life. With Mary, we made things up as we went. It was as though she was getting ready to start a new life and the past never existed. As gratifying as it was to help her get out of the funk she was in, I worried that I might not be giving her the right advice. I was only telling her what I would do. I was a decent person and all, but I certainly wasn't qualified to help her make life-altering decisions. But then again, who really was qualified? Did I need a degree in counseling to tell a woman that her husband was a big, fat, smelly dog turd that has been baking in the hot July sun? Did I have to be a parent to foresee that Mary's stepdaughter was going to grow up to be a lonely woman if she didn't learn how to treat people with respect, especially the woman who mothered her when hers decided she didn't want to anymore?

"I auditioned for that play," Mary said, starting things off.

Assuming the worst, I replied, "Don't be discouraged if you don't get a part this time. They have plays all the time. The next one…"

"I got a part!" she shouted.

"That's wonderful! I am so proud of you! I thought for sure that paper would end up in the garbage."

Mary auditioning for the play was another step toward rediscovering herself. She desperately needed to find the Mary that was confident enough in her abilities to get up on stage again after all these years. I was truly proud of her. Even though I had known her for only a short while, I felt like a mother bird watching her baby spread its wings for the first time. Mary was leaving the nest, if only for a few hours a night.

"You'll never guess who encouraged me in my decision."

"If it means choosing between your husband and stepdaughter, then you're right. I'll never guess."

"I've painted a pretty awful picture of them, haven't I?"

"You were venting your frustrations. I'm sure they're both delightful people in their own way," I said, seeing the guilt on her face. I didn't feel guilty for not liking them even though I didn't know them. I didn't want to know them. I had heard enough to know that their character was missing a few of the essential traits, kindness being one of them.

"After I left here last week with that audition schedule in my hand, I drove straight home, tossed it in the mail pile with the rest of the junk, and went right back to doing the same menial tasks I did every day. I didn't give it a second thought. Then Stacy came home, rummaged through the pile looking for who knows what, and pulled out the clipping. 'What's this?' she asked. I replied with a typical short answer, 'A friend gave it to me.' To my surprise, she didn't just walk away. She instead asked more questions. As I listed off the plays I had been in before I met her father, she was actually being attentive. It has been years since she's wanted to hear what I had to say. Come to find out she's always wanted to be in a school production, but was worried that her snooty friends might make fun of her, which is understandable. The drama geeks aren't appreciated in every school."

I nodded in agreement.

"When I thought our conversation was over, Stacy asked me if I was going to audition. I told her I didn't think I had it in me anymore to get back up on stage. Her next comment was what sent me over the edge and to that audition. She simply said, 'Well, you should. Why not?'"

"Some of your smarts must have worn off on her."

"Maybe I should get some credit for that," Mary said, her face glowing with pride. "So, anyway, I did it. I went into that audition with as much confidence as I could muster up and gave a good enough performance to land a supporting role."

"Good for you, Mary."

"I have you to thank for this."

"I'll only take partial credit. I didn't do anything but ask a few questions, maybe give a few suggestions. You decided to participate in life."

"And it feels so good."

"What was your husband's reaction?" I asked.

Mary's eyes grew large like I had asked her about a ghost in her closet.

"I haven't told him yet," she said, lowering her gaze.

"Hmm" was all I murmured. I didn't want to press the issue. She had made it clear that she was sticking by her man no matter how smelly and rotten he was. Nancy's arrival saved us from further discussion.

"Ladies, are we ready?" Nancy asked.

"Are you here to take Mary out for a celebratory lunch?" I asked.

"Aren't you coming?"

"I didn't know I was invited."

"Didn't you get my text?"

"No," I said, laughing. This wasn't the first time she had forgotten to tell me about something. I sometimes wondered if all that clinging and clanging in the Las Vegas casinos permanently damaged her brain or if she really was that ditzy. It was probably a combination of the two.

Nancy and I continued to jokingly squabble over her communication skills, but in the end I was thankful to be included in their plans. It was an honor to dine with two confident women celebrating their reemergence into society. It was also a good way to keep my mind off my upcoming trip to Bergan.

38

"You better call me if anything happens," Kendall ordered.

I called Kendall after eating a late dinner all by my lonesome. I still wasn't that hungry after my unscheduled lunch date with Mary and Nancy. The intentions for my call were to see if she was feeling better, however, using her mommy magic she somehow turned the conversation around by badgering me about Kevin. I made one small slip-up and she was all over me, which led me to tell her everything about our unexpected night together. By the way she was bossing me around and getting all up in my business, I knew the overindulgence in alcohol had evacuated her system. I quickly decided I liked her better hungover.

"What, pray tell, do you plan to do from two hundred miles away?" I seriously wanted to hear this.

"I just want to know if I should worry about you."

"That'll do wonders for the both of us."

"You know what I mean," Kendall scolded.

"Okay, we'll be in contact. You'll be like my virtual copilot. Happy now?" I walked past my front window to glance at the setting sun. Panic set in, however, when I noticed the car parked in my driveway.

I dodged out of sight and into the entryway. Cutting Kendall's lecture short, I said, "There's someone parked in my driveway."

"Who is it?" she asked.

"I don't know. It looks like the same car that was here the night I went out with Sam."

"Do you think you should call the police? What if it's Michael or his son?"

"Michael drives an SUV. I'm going to try to get a better look," I said, inching my way back over to the window. Once again the sun was a hindrance. All I could make out was the silhouette of a man wearing a baseball cap. Well, that narrowed it down.

"You should call the police, Kody."

"Let me keep an eye on him for a minute. Maybe it's someone that's lost."

"Or maybe it's someone who wants you lost."

"Way to keep it positive, Kendall."

"I'm positive it's a serial rapist coming to get you."

"Stop it already. I live alone, remember? Do you want me to be even more paranoid?"

"I'm sorry. You should really..."

"He's getting out of his car," I interrupted, jetting back to my hideout. What if Kendall was right? What if it was a rapist coming to get me?

Ding-dong.

Rapists didn't ring doorbells.

"Kendall, what do I do?" I asked, assuming she heard the doorbell."

"Don't answer it. Pretend you're not home."

The house was lit up like a Christmas tree and the television projected through the front window. "I don't think that's going to work."

"Don't you have a peephole in your door? Look through that."

Nothing like the obvious. I stood up and rolled out of the corner I had squeezed into, still doubting the concept that peepholes were installed to look from the inside out and not the other way around. All the while, Kendall repeatedly asked who was outside my door.

I breathed a sigh of relief when the man on my front porch came into focus.

"It's Paul," I finally answered.

Without hesitation, Kendall ordered, "You better call me later. I'm talking as soon as he leaves."

I hung up the phone and rustled the door open.

Paul spoke first.

"I'm sorry to come here without calling first. I went for a drive and this is where I ended up. Is this okay?"

Standing at my door, hands fidgeting, he looked like that same boy from years ago who didn't know what to do or say when I told him I was pregnant. It was that same look of fear and hesitation, like he wanted to say the right words, but wasn't sure what those words were.

"It's fine," I said, stepping back to let him in. "You scared me sitting out in my driveway like that. I was talking on the phone with Kendall and she almost had me persuaded to call the police."

Paul's eyes widened. "I'm glad you didn't. There was just a bit of a battle going on in the car," he smirked. "I thought the two sides of me were going to throw blows, but we somehow worked everything out. It's all good now."

I had to laugh. I remembered how he used to beat himself up over having to make the smallest decisions in high school. The battle to participate in senior skip day was one for the record books. The conversation we had the night before was agonizing. To me it wasn't that big of a deal, but Paul acted as if it might show up on his permanent record.

"I would say we should go out on the deck to talk, but the mosquitoes are really bad."

Paul held out his arms that were covered in red welts. "I know. I had the window down out there."

"A lot happened out in my driveway," I laughed, walking into the kitchen. I grabbed a couple of beers from the fridge and handed him one, which he graciously accepted. "Everything okay at home? Is your mom not folding your underwear right or something?"

"You remember that," Paul chuckled. "No, she folds them and the rest of my laundry just like I remembered. She's even cooking all my favorite meals. My dad is the same too, except now he's teaching me the hardware business. Before, he didn't want me anywhere near the place. All in all, I would say life couldn't be any better."

Paul's words weren't convincing. There was an emptiness in his eyes. It was obvious he needed a friend to talk to. I was shocked that he chose me of all people. We had made amends the other weekend, but I knew for a fact that some of his best friends still lived at home.

"You're not that happy to be back, are you?" I asked as we sat down on opposite ends of the couch.

"I'm happy. Of course I'm happy. I'm a newly divorced man living back at home with my parents sleeping in the same bedroom I grew up in. Why wouldn't I be happy?" Paul tipped back his head and sucked down half of his beer.

"That is a charmed life," I said sarcastically. "It's completely better than never having been married and living alone while the rest of your friends are married with children. Now that is something special."

We laughed at how pathetic we both sounded. Neither of our lives had yet to turn out like we expected. I was still waiting for my prince charming while he was picking up the pieces after his princess found a new and improved prince.

"Still haven't found the one, huh, Kody?" Paul asked, finishing his beer.

"I'm still looking" was all I said as I got up to get him another one.

"I wish I would have been pickier. Shannon and I eloped after only six months of dating. I thought we were a match made in heaven. Every couple thinks that in the beginning."

"I usually find something wrong with the guy within two weeks. Six months is impressive."

A smile spread across his face until he started telling me about his ex-wife. "The last couple of years we just sort of separated, both mentally and physically. We didn't have anything to talk about, nor did we try to do anything about it. Before long, she had an affair. I forgave her, blaming myself for letting it happen. The second time though was a different story. It was with a friend of mine and they kept it a secret from me for months. There's nothing worse than having someone you love keep that kind of secret from you. I felt like such a dumbass for not catching on to it. It never once occurred to me that they were doing anything behind my back."

"I'm sorry to hear that."

"You never cheated on me, did you? With Jeremy? I've always kind of wondered that."

My jaw dropped and my eyes narrowed. Was that why he was here, to find out if I cheated on him in high school?

"Are you serious right now? I never cheated on you. Jeremy was a friend. He was your friend too if you remember correctly. I hope you didn't come all this way to ask me that. You could have saved yourself a trip if that's the case."

"Geez, Kody. No, of course that's not why I'm here. I came here to see you, to hang out with a friend. I don't care if you cheated on me." He held his hands out in front of his face as if to block a punch. "I know you didn't and I thank you for that." He sighed. "Can we start over? Can I try coming in again? Please? I didn't come here to start a fight. I really want us to be friends again. I've missed you. Dancing with you the other night reminded me of what a kind and genuine person you are and that's the type of person I need in my life right now."

Paul's eyes pleaded with me to forgive him. He didn't come here to question me about Jeremy. His words weren't meant to harm me. They were more meant to heal him. He needed to know that when he and I were together my heart belonged solely to him. He needed to believe that love didn't always involve secrets.

"I don't want to start this night over because I don't want to be freaked out again by seeing some stranger parked in my driveway," I half smiled. "Speaking of, have you done that before?"

"What? Park in your driveway?"

"Yeah."

"Just one other time. You weren't home." Looking perplexed, he asked, "Why? Did a neighbor tell you about a suspicious man lurking around your house?"

"Something like that," I said, not wanting to mention that I was out on a date, a dreadful one at that. "Well, you're here now. I'm here."

Paul leaned back, seemingly more relaxed.

"I have more beer in the fridge and I think there are a couple of bottles of wine in the cupboard. I say we enjoy the present company and drink our worries away. No harm in that, right?"

"No harm at all," he said, raising his beer bottle. I raised mine and we toasted to friendship.

The rest of the evening was a bit of a blur as was expected by my proclamation of being well stocked with alcohol. The drinks flowed and so did the stories from our past. I never had so much fun talking about other people. He knew quirky things about our high school classmates that I had no idea about. For instance, word never got out, not to me at least, that Lenny Hurt had a third nipple on his back. Why didn't I know that? That's important information in high school. Paul also knew that Cory Brimm had two moms, which was cool, but again, how did I not know that? We didn't bother to touch on our own lives. That would have been too real, too personal. Being enlightened on what I never knew and talking about other's screw ups seemed more enjoyable. It was almost too enjoyable.

I woke up the next morning with a dry mouth and a pounding headache. Wine did that to me every time. Paul was still passed out on the couch. Around one in the morning I watched his eyes glaze over and then close as I told him about the time in middle school when some friends and I sneaked out of my house to throw eggs at another friend's house. The rebellious act completely backfired on us though because her parents caught us and called our parents on the spot. As no surprise, we spent the next morning scrubbing dried egg off their house and the next two weeks being grounded.

"Paul," I whispered, nudging his shoulder. No response. "Paul," I said louder. His eyes popped open. A look of bewilderment spread across his face. Can you say disoriented?

"What time is it?" he asked.

"Just after seven."

After a few seconds to recollect his location, Paul's eyes fell closed once again. He couldn't have been feeling awfully well either. He drank two to my one for a while. Once we ran out of beer we switched to wine, which if I remember the saying correctly, we should be feeling fine today. The saying said nothing about quantity, however. On my way into the living room, I passed at least three bottles of wine and countless beer bottles. From the looks of it, I had a small gathering of friends over, not just a party for two.

"I can't move," he whispered.

"Do you need to go to work or at least call your dad?" I asked, feeling like we were still in high school. I couldn't remember the last time I had asked a friend if they needed to check in with their parents.

Moaning and groaning, Paul lifted himself into a seated position. His eyes remained closed as he patted down his pockets looking for his cell phone. Having located his phone, his eyes squinted open just enough to push the right buttons. The whole scene was quite comical. I would have laughed out loud if I thought it wasn't going to make my head hurt worse.

Paul's conversation with his dad was short and sweet, "Dad, I'm not coming in today." End of call. He laid back down on the couch without so much as a word to me. Not feeling up to being anyone's babysitter, I gladly went back to bed. There was no one I needed to call. I would only have to offer an apology to anyone who stopped by the office. My luck, no apology would be required.

Hours later, I awoke to Paul's smiling face staring down at me. Isn't it weird how you always know when someone is staring at you?

"I'm leaving," he said, his hand covering his mouth in an attempt to shield me from his morning breath. "I'll call you." Before departing, he leaned down and kissed me on the forehead.

"Okay," I said as I watched him leave my bedroom. I waited to hear the front door close before rolling out of bed. Shuffling to the bathroom, I caught a whiff of something delicious. The smell of grease and bacon permeated through the hallway. My nose followed the scent to the kitchen where my eyes feasted on the fast-food bag on the counter. I didn't have to open the bag to know what was inside. Paul knew me too well.

39

To: kodyburkoff@inyourwords.com
From: sad_dad1@gmail.com
Subject: It's out of my control

I'm no example for my son. It's not like I have a choice in all of this. My anger, my compulsion, controls me. I lost a daughter for crying out loud. I lost a piece of me that I'll never ever get back. You don't know how I feel. You said yourself that you've never experienced loss like this. Neither have the Knutson's. Their family is all intact, for now. Gabe tries to understand, but it's different. He didn't watch his wife give birth to a precious baby girl. He didn't see her take her first breath. There is nothing in the world like holding a newborn baby, especially one that you had a hand in creating.

You should stay out of this, Kody. Snuggle up tight with your cat and be thankful for what you have. Be thankful that your future is bright and that you have family and friends that love you. Some of us don't have that anymore. We've scared everyone away. Even if I did get better, even if I did seek help like you say, I'll still be lonely. I'll still be that guy who lost his daughter. I'll never be the same, which is a shame because I used to be a fun guy. I was the teacher all the kids requested. I was the dad who made an elephant sound with his mouth and charged after the herd of children pretending to graze in our backyard. I was the husband who told his wife he loved her before kissing her goodnight. I was all those things and more.

Now though, I'm nothing but a deranged man eager to even the playing field. I know what you're thinking, "That won't solve your problems." I know that. Killing Peder will only create more havoc for me and my family. I'm not stupid. I've tried rationalizing with myself. It doesn't work. Julia's smiling face wins every time. She's the one I'm fighting for. She's the one who can't right the wrong for herself.

I've also considered joining Julia. If that doesn't stop my compulsion, I don't know what will. I picture the two of us walking hand in hand like we used to do along the lake shore when she was a toddler. She can fill me in on what I missed while we were apart. I'll listen attentively, soaking up the sound of her voice. It would be wonderful to see her again, to hear her again. There's only one problem: Peder would remain a murderer and a survivor. I don't know if I can let that happen.

sad dad

40

"I didn't kill your daughter!" I wanted to shout out the window at the top of my lungs. Julia's dad stood on the sidewalk in front of our house staring at the wood and glass, every once in a while swiping at his face to knock down the tears. I knew today, the anniversary of Julia's death, was going to be bad, but I never thought he would plant himself in our front yard in broad daylight. He did conveniently wait until my parents left for work. That was smart of him. Plus, his being here was for my eyes only. Well, my eyes and those of the rest of the neighborhood who were undoubtedly questioning his sanity. It was only a matter of time before one of them called the police. I wasn't going to be the one. My dad gave me strict orders not to call them. Instead, I was supposed to call him, but I didn't want to do that either. He has had about enough of the police and other people questioning our family's safety. My dad considered it his duty, his obligation to keep our family safe, even from people as emotionally damaged as Julia's dad.

My dad must have given the same orders to someone else in the neighborhood because when I poked my head up over the top of the couch his truck was rumbling up the driveway. He pulled in only far enough to be out of the road before exiting the truck to confront

Michael Calhoun. My dad was all up in his face, even jabbing him in the chest a few times. If he thought he could get away with it, I knew he would have thrown a punch. Mr. Calhoun didn't budge. He barely even flinched. I couldn't make out any words from either man because of the hum of the air conditioner, but from what I saw, my dad wasn't giving Mr. Calhoun much of a chance to speak. I sat peering over the back of the couch only long enough to read Mr. Calhoun's lips. He mouthed, "He killed her."

I ducked back down into my hiding spot. I couldn't watch anymore. He was wrong. I didn't kill her. I would never kill anyone. It was an accident, a horrible, terrible accident. Why couldn't he accept that? I'm no monster. I don't go around killing people and I don't go around stalking innocent kids either. I feared that I was going to have to spend the rest of my life defending what I didn't do. Was that fair? It was about as fair as having the image of Julia's dead body finding its way into my thoughts uninvited on a daily basis. The dead stare was what got to me the most. I had never seen anything like it. I had never felt such emptiness while looking at someone. Julia was gone in an instant. The body that housed her was all that remained.

The front door slammed shut. I was in trouble.

"Why didn't you call me?" my dad asked, still flushed with rage.

Before answering him I poked my head back up to see a police officer escorting Mr. Calhoun across the street.

"Is he going to jail?" I asked.

"No. He's being taken home. Why didn't you call me? I thought we had a deal. Now the police are here and our neighborhood looks like a spectacle."

"He wasn't doing anything but standing there. I didn't want to bother you for just that."

My dad rubbed his right hand over the goatee he had worn on his face for as long as I could remember. He wasn't happy with my answer.

"You know what day it is, right?" he asked, trying to keep his calm.

"Yes sir."

"Then you know that of all days to call me when something like this happens, today is the day. I know you're almost a man now, but it's still my job to protect you. And from the looks of you hiding out on the couch, you had no intention of doing anything about him on your own."

"I figured he'd just go away."

"You figured he'd just go away." He placed his hands on his waist and puffed out his chest. "Has he ever gone away over the course of this last year?"

I shook my head.

"He'll never go away unless we make him go away."

My dad moved past me to stand in front of the window where two police officers remained talking in the road. Mr. Calhoun sat in the back seat of one of the squad cars looking straight ahead.

"What are you going to do?" I finally asked.

"I don't know yet, but I do know that our family can't tolerate Mr. Calhoun's behavior much longer." With that said, he stomped back to his bedroom and closed the door.

I didn't leave the couch the rest of the day, except for a bathroom break and a trip to the kitchen. My dad didn't leave the bedroom until mid afternoon and then he left without saying so much as a word to me. What was going through his mind? What did he have planned? He wasn't the kind of guy to let you in on any secrets. He bottled a lot of things up. Like when my grandma died, he barely showed any emotion. It's just the way he was. Emotions were weaknesses to him, which was probably why he treated me like a little kid still. I wasn't the tough guy he made himself out to be. He thought my depression was a load of crap. That's what I heard him tell my mom. But he didn't see Julia's eyes. He didn't make someone die.

41

"Did you see the curtain move?" I asked Kevin, watching every slight movement coming from the Calhoun residence.

"It might be the air conditioner starting up. Lower your window so you can listen."

I forced my window down, although I questioned my actions because it was safe to assume that most people were using their air conditioners since it was still eighty degrees at eleven o'clock at night. Let's not forget that the humidity was so thick you could cut it with a knife. Hmm. Did that saying go along with humidity or tension? Either way, I figured it was appropriate being that Kevin and I were waiting for Michael or Gabe to make a move, and we had been at each other's throats off and on since leaving Belmont. Kevin overheard Kendall ask me about Paul on the phone and he was mad that I wouldn't tell him who Paul was. That was a secret I still intended to keep.

We had already driven past the Knutson residence and sure enough the whole family was home. There were two cars in the driveway and because of their lack of curtain use we could see that someone was up watching *Storage Wars*. It certainly didn't seem as though they were the least bit worried about having a visitor in the middle of the night.

My assumption had been correct. The outdoors was filled with the hum of electricity.

"This neighborhood looks a lot like the one I grew up in," Kevin revealed.

"Really?" I said.

"Yeah, it was a great place to grow up. My mom and I lived in the same two bedroom house for years. It wasn't much bigger than what I'm living in now."

"Sounds quaint."

"It was. I remember for my tenth birthday she surprised me by painting my bedroom purple and gold for the Vikings. It was around that time that I became a die-hard fan."

"That's cute. My room was blue and gold, our school colors. I painted it myself though."

"Figures."

"What's that supposed to mean?" I asked.

"Only that you prefer to do most things yourself. You don't exactly play by anyone else's rules."

Here we go again. Did he really think I didn't play by anyone else's rules? Well, he was wrong. I played by other people's rules. Not everything had to be my way. I mean, I preferred to do things my way, but if it didn't work out, it didn't work out. Damn, he frustrated me.

"What else was so wonderful about your house, Mr. Sassypants?"

"We've resorted to name calling, huh?" Kevin laughed.

"I don't like to be told that I'm bossy." I wasn't laughing.

"I never said bossy."

"Well, you might as well have. I can read between the lines."

"You look hot when you're angry," he said with a wink. "Read between those lines."

"Honestly, Kevin, you are too much. And I'm not reading between those lines because this is not the time to discuss your desires."

"You never want to discuss my desires," he said, repositioning himself to face the side window.

What a pouter. This was neither the time nor the place to discuss anyone's desires. If it was desire he wished to discuss, it should be Peder's desire to stay alive on the anniversary of Julia's death. I didn't want to take time for Kevin's selfish display so I let him sulk in silence, which led us through almost a half hour. The silent standoff was forgotten once Michael's garage door opened.

"Down," I yelled.

"We need to see where he's going," Kevin yelled back, his eyes peeking just over the steering wheel.

Not wanting him to see something I didn't, I inched my way back up the seat just in time to see Michael backing out. As expected, he turned the SUV in the direction of the Knutson's. Because we had anticipated this move, we made sure to park along the street on the opposite side. It wasn't as if Michael could see us anyway. The moon was but a sliver in the sky and the street lights were scarce in the older neighborhood.

As discussed, we held tight in the vehicle waiting for Michael to get far enough ahead so that he didn't notice us following him. We also knew that in only a matter of seconds Gabe would dart out from around the side of the house.

Five. Four. Three. Two. One. There he went sprinting across the neighbor's yard disappearing into the darkness.

"Let's go," I urged Kevin. Michael was about to turn right up ahead. Once again, it was a movement we had anticipated.

Kevin started the car. "I'm going to drive with the lights off."

"Okay." I couldn't believe this was finally happening. Planning to stake out someone's home was one thing, but actually doing it was a whole other story. And then to take it one step further by following them to a place we knew there was danger.

With the headlights off, we drove down the street and took a right where Michael had only seconds ago. His SUV was just up ahead, but there was no sight of Gabe anywhere. I took it upon myself to keep an eye on him since Kevin's job was to keep his eyes on the road and on Michael, which was difficult in the dark. Gabe was probably quick enough to stay closer to his dad's vehicle, and because he was a teenager it was safe to assume he was also fairly decent at not being seen when he didn't want to be. Remember those days of trying to blend in at the school dances? I felt like I did a good job of it, or was that simply my perception at the time?

We anticipated one more right turn at the corner with the house that had a bashed-up derby car in the driveway. Instead, Michael drove straight.

"Maybe he'll turn at the next corner," I said.

Kevin remained silent as he continued to follow Michael's lead. It wasn't like him to be so quiet in a tense situation such as this one. Usually when he was nervous he rambled on, filling the air with what-if statements.

"Are you scared?" I asked.

"Yeah, but it's okay. This is the right thing to do."

It *was* the right thing to do. If all worked out as planned, we would follow Michael to the Knutson's where we would flag down a police officer that was driving by as requested by Investigator Dunn. If it didn't work out quite that way, I was willing to make myself known to Michael while Kevin called the police. Either way, our main objective was to keep Peder out of harm's way, and subsequently stop Michael from doing something he would later regret.

"I'm scared too," I said, putting my hand on Kevin's thigh. My polite gesture didn't even last long enough for my palm to get sweaty. Kevin pointed at Michael's SUV.

"He's not turning, Kody. He should have turned at that next corner if he was planning to drive around the block. What do we do? Should we keep following him? Maybe this is when we call the police and let them handle it? What about Gabe?"

This was the Kevin I knew. "Keep your calm, Kevin," I said, taking in our surroundings. "We're at the edge of town already. And look, there's a speed limit sign up ahead. It's about to change to fifty-five." In a panic, I checked the side mirror for any sign of Gabe. Sure enough, the silhouette of a figure stood at the edge of the road several yards behind us. Kevin saw him too.

"We should go back to get him. He might know where his father is going," Kevin said.

"That's a good idea. Let's do it quick though. We don't want to lose sight of Michael and my guess is that Gabe will take off once he sees us closing in on him," I replied. "You wore your sneakers, right?"

Gabe didn't move though. He stood as still as a statue as we backed the car up until we were next to him. His bewildered eyes met mine as I lowered the window.

"I'm Kody Burkoff, Gabe. Do you know where your dad is going?" I asked, watching Michael's taillights disappear into the night.

He shook his head.

"This is really important. If you think you can help us, you need to get in the car now. We've already lost sight of him," I said, pointing into the horizon.

With little hesitation, Gabe jumped into the back seat of Kevin's Honda Civic. The three of us took off down the road, this time turning on the headlights. There wasn't exactly a steady stream of cars on the road this late at night, which was also why it didn't take us long to catch up with our target. Michael's SUV was just around the bend. Kevin kept his distance.

"I'm Kevin by the way," Kevin said, looking at Gabe through the rearview mirror.

I turned my head around slightly to see Gabe's reaction. He opted to ignore Kevin's greeting and continued to stare out the window. He wasn't ready to talk to us. I couldn't blame him. He had to be wondering why we were here and what we planned to do with his father, or better yet, where his father was going. I sensed that he knew we were here to help, and although this was an unconventional way to do it, it was how he was used to dealing with situations.

We continued to follow Michael for several minutes before he slowed down to make yet another right-hand turn, this time to leave the highway.

"Do you know where we are, Gabe?" Kevin asked.

Again, Gabe shook his head.

"Cut the lights, Kevin," I ordered before he turned to follow Michael.

Kevin did as I asked before swerving to the side of the road. He didn't look happy. For privacy, he turned the radio on and the volume up. "Do you know how dangerous this is, Kody? I don't think this is a good idea anymore."

"What could go wrong?" I asked. "If we stay far enough away, Michael won't even know we're here." I nodded my head back, gesturing toward Gabe. "Being that he's out here by himself, I worry that he might take his own life."

"More reason to get the hell out of here. The last thing that kid needs to see is his father splattered all over the inside of his SUV."

Kevin had a point, but I wasn't ready to call it quits quite yet. "We can't give up now," I pleaded. "We came all this way to try to fix things for the Calhoun family and the Knutson's, and if we leave now nothing changes. I'll still wake up every morning wondering if Peder is okay, if Michael is going to send me another e-mail, or if Gabe is going to grow up to be as demented as his father. Please, Kevin. Let's keep following him just a little while longer."

"There wasn't a chance of me ever winning this argument, was there?" he asked, looking into the darkness ahead instead of at me.

"There shouldn't be a winner or a loser in this argument," I said under my breath.

Whether he heard my last comment or he simply gave in to my demands, Kevin pulled out onto the gravel road to follow Michael's diminishing taillights. As we made our way into the darkness, I glanced back at Gabe. He sat hunched over, strands of hair hanging in his eyes that were glossy from a lack of sleep and most likely worry for his father's well-being. Even if Gabe hadn't heard what Kevin and I said, he knew what we feared the most. It was the same fear he lived with every day since his sister's death.

It was virtually impossible to see the road ahead. Kevin ought to have been driving blindfolded for as well as we were able to see out the windshield. Then, as expected, the unexpected occurred. The road vanished from beneath the car and in an instant we took a nosedive—fast. I threw my arms out in front of me as if my strength was enough to stop gravity from hurling us to lower ground. Fortunately, we didn't fall far. A dim reflection on the surface in front of me, along with the sound of running water, gave way to the conclusion that we had landed in a shallow stream.

"Everyone okay?" I asked, hanging forward in my seatbelt. I looked to my left to see Kevin still gripping the steering wheel.

"I'm okay," Kevin said.

Afraid to move, I asked Gabe directly, "Gabe, are you okay? Please answer me if you can."

"I'm fine," he said with irritation in his voice.

I was irritated too, but more relieved than anything. This idea of mine to save someone's life was not intended for anyone riding in the same vehicle as me.

"I'm going to open my..." Kevin started to say, only to be interrupted by Gabe's door opening and him splashing into the water.

"Gabe!" Kevin and I shouted in unison. Apparently he wasn't worried that the car might tip to one side if one of us shifted our weight or got out of the car.

"Its fine," Gabe said in a non-melodramatic tone. "The car is leaning against the bridge. It isn't going anywhere. You guys can get out."

I wanted to trust him. I really did.

"You go first, Kody," Kevin said.

"No, you go first," I argued. "The car is leaning in your direction."

"Exactly, that's why if you get out first, my weight will keep the car in place. If I get out first, your weight might send the car tumbling on its side."

"How much do you think I weigh, Kevin?"

"Kody, you seriously can't think this is a good time to discuss your weight."

"I didn't think my weight deserved a discussion."

"Get out!" Kevin shouted, with glaring eyes. He would have shown his teeth too if this were a vampire story.

"Okay, okay, Captain Friendly," I said, making sure to get the last word. I am who I am regardless of my location.

Very carefully I opened my door and then unbuckled the seatbelt to gently lower myself down into the water. Okay, so that wasn't exactly how it happened. Once that seatbelt came undone, for some reason I had one leg out of the car while the other one remained inside. Needless to say, I ended up submerging most of my body in the fresh, gurgling brook that smelled like a fresh load of laundry. Well, not exactly, but that's the story I'm planning to tell people.

Kevin's exit was far more graceful. Damn him. I was hoping to have company in my misery.

After I shook off the excess water I was carrying in my cargo shorts, the three of us met under what we learned was a small bridge, without a railing mind you, over a culvert that ran along an intersecting road. Gabe was his usual quiet self, sitting as far away from us as he could get. I wanted to snuggle up to Kevin to steal some of his warmth, but he was having no part of it. Anger still consumed him.

"Now what?" Kevin asked.

I was just about to ask the same question. Instead, I felt obligated to form an answer and the one that was at the tip of my tongue was not going to make anyone happy.

"Let's walk over to Michael," I answered.

"I knew you were going to say that," Kevin grumbled. "Don't you think we should call the police? My car is basically standing on its head and we have no idea where we are."

I said nothing. Gabe was also silent.

"Where's your phone?" Kevin barked.

"It's in my pocket," I barked back, feeling for the hunk of metal and plastic in my wet shorts. Wet shorts. Wet phone. Dead phone.

After trying everything I could think of to make the phone work, I reluctantly said, "It won't turn on."

"You're kidding me? Gabe, you must have a phone on you," Kevin said.

"Mine's at home."

"What? I didn't think teenagers left home without them," Kevin said, redirecting his anger at Gabe instead of me.

Gabe looked at Kevin and said, "I'm not like other teenagers."

That shut him up.

"What about you, Kevin, where's your phone?" I asked snidely.

"I didn't bring it," he said, walking away from us.

"I didn't think computer geeks left home without them," I mimicked.

"Don't get all sassy with me. I dropped it yesterday and didn't have time to get it replaced. I figured you having a phone would suffice for the both of us."

Kevin and I continued to squabble over whose fault it was for not having a cell phone or some other form of communication on this trip, which once again reminded me of why we broke up in the first place. We were undeniably more like brother and sister than boyfriend and girlfriend. There were more moments that I despised him than lusted after him.

"I'm going after my dad," Gabe interrupted, immediately halting our bickering. Before Kevin and I had a chance to argue with him, Gabe had climbed halfway up the embankment. We quickly followed.

Once on ground level, we were able to see the faint glow of headlights reflecting off an assumingly abandoned building about a half mile ahead and to our left. It was hard to tell what else was over there from this distance, especially with the increasing number of trees and the lack of human inhabitants in the surrounding area. If there was ever something you wanted hidden, this was the perfect spot. What did Michael have planned on the anniversary of his daughter's death? Why was he here? The possibilities were endless, of course, but committing suicide was the one logical answer that stood out to me.

Silently, the three of us, with Gabe in the lead, followed the gravel road leading to Michael. Even though the night was warm, the summer breeze sent a shiver down my spine. It didn't help that I was still wet from my less than graceful exit from Kevin's car, although I had a feeling that even if I was bone dry I would have felt the same way. I couldn't escape the mental image of finding Michael's lifeless body with half of his face blown to pieces. I wondered if Gabe or Kevin was thinking the same thing. We all knew he kept a gun in his glove compartment.

Our pace slowed as we closed in on the SUV. The sound of our footsteps filled the eerie silence. Gabe was now walking in between Kevin and me. He was either beginning to trust us or he didn't want to be the first one at the scene.

Without notice, the SUV's reverse lights ignited and the vehicle shot backward. Michael was on the move again, which was both good and bad. Good in that he was still alive, but bad in that he was probably now heading to the Knutson's and we had no way to stop him.

Not wanting to be seen, we instinctively took off in a dead sprint into the woods lining the gravel road. Well, technically my sprint was more like a fast jog. I trailed Kevin, dodging behind the first available tree that was large enough to hide me. I tried to calm my breathing while peeking around the side of the tree to watch Michael drive away. Once again, all I saw was taillights.

When it was evident that Michael wasn't turning back, I came out from my hiding spot, making one final silent plea, *Please be on your way home, Michael.*

Appearing at my side was Kevin. "I wonder if he'll notice my car. He obviously didn't see us creeping up behind him. There was barely enough time to get out of the way."

"My guess is he's in his own little world right now. I only hope the police are circling the Knutson's block. I have a feeling they won't want to miss out on the excitement," I replied. Hearing and then seeing Gabe walk past, I added, "Since we're here, we might as well go and check out that old building he was parked in front of and look for clues."

"Okay, Velma," Kevin muttered under his breath.

If looks could kill, he would be dead right now.

Upon further inspection, with the moon as our only source of light, the building was just as I had suspected. It was an old log cabin that someone must have inhabited at one time, perhaps as a seasonal hunting lodge. It wasn't especially big and it didn't have any modern-day facilities, which I was bummed about. Squatting in the woods really wasn't my thing. The door was missing a handle and some of the glass in the windows was long gone. There were a few crumpled aluminum cans left behind and that was about it.

"I don't see anything in here," Kevin said.

"There has to be a reason why Michael was here. I can't imagine him coming all this way just to sit here and reflect, or perhaps in Michael's case, to justify a reason to live."

"Let's keep looking then. There's got to be more to this."

Before we took another step, Gabe's voice echoed among the trees.

"Help! I'm down here!" he shouted.

Kevin and I followed Gabe's cries for help. The poor kid was completely freaking out. I had never heard him say more than a few words at one time. Using Gabe's voice as a guide, we crept along the uneven ground stepping over the tall brush to avoid getting stuck with thorns. It didn't take us long to find him. He was only a few yards into the woods on the far side of the cabin. When we reached our destination, my feet sunk into loose soil along the edge of a huge hole. Michael must have been preparing to plant a large tree in the woods. It's your prerogative to disagree.

"Kevin, get him out of there," I shouted, freaking out a bit myself. "Gabe, we're here. We're going to help you."

Gabe's screams downgraded to whimpers. I felt impelled to say soothing words to calm him down while Kevin lay along the edge of the hole that I estimated to be about five feet long by two feet wide, and then at least six feet deep. With Gabe being right around my height at five feet six, there was no way he would be able to hoist himself out on his own.

Michael had obviously spent a lot of time digging this hole. I suppose it was quite therapeutic being out in these woods plotting the death and burial of the person who took something so valuable from him. It was in the perfect location too. The dilapidated building hid the site from any vehicle that happened to drive along the gravel road, and then the thick brush added extra camouflage. There was no other reason for anyone to be out here. No other reason but revenge.

"Grab my hands and I'll pull you out," Kevin instructed.

Gabe did as he was told and with a few tugs he was back on level ground. I quickly grabbed a hold of him, wiped his tears away, and told him everything was going to be okay. I didn't have many motherly instincts, but I knew when someone needed a hug. Falling into an empty grave was the perfect scenario. Gabe didn't fight me off one bit. He clung to me while his body shook with fear.

Finally letting go of Gabe, but still staying close, I said what we were all thinking, "I have a feeling I know who that grave is meant for."

"So do I," Gabe said.

42

"Get dressed," my dad snapped, barging into my room at just after one in the morning. "Meet me in the backyard."

I rubbed the sleep out of my eyes and did as I was told. The scowl on his face told me that this wasn't the time to question his authority. I was mad at myself for being woken up to begin with. My intention was to stay awake all night so that I could surprise Michael when he returned for a visit. I knew he would be back, especially tonight. My plan was to return his stare when he peered through my window, although with tonight being such a special occasion, I wondered if I would see more than a pair of eyes.

The back porch light wasn't on so when I approached the french doors in the dining room I saw the faint shadow of my dad standing next to the shed in our backyard. I quietly left the house so as not to wake my mom and ventured off into the darkness to meet up with him.

"Grab a shovel and follow me," he said.

Hesitating briefly, I grabbed the newer of the two shovels and followed him around the shed. We continued through the back gate in the wood fence to his idling truck parked in the alley. With my shovel in hand, I made the safe assumption that we weren't going on a late-night fishing excursion. I wouldn't let my imagination travel any further than that for fear that the nightmare I had been living for the past year was no longer a worry I needed to have.

"I want you to see something before we get started," he said, leading me to the back of the truck. The vinyl cover was stretched over the bed so I had to wait until he opened the tailgate to see the surprise. Before revealing the contents of the truck, he said, "I want you to know that I love you and your mother dearly. As the man of the house, it is my job to protect the two of you. I had hoped it wouldn't come down to this, but I had no other choice."

He opened the tailgate and it wasn't immediately clear to me what he had stowed in there. Seeing my confusion, my dad reached in and pulled out a man's hand from the cover of darkness.

"Dad!" I yelled before he clapped a hand over my mouth.

"Don't you start screaming like a little girl. This man was going to kill you tonight. You should thank me for saving your life."

"That's Michael Calhoun?" I rubbed my hands through my hair in disbelief.

"You're damn right it is. I caught him outside your window. He had a gun with him too. I was ready for him this time. He didn't even know what hit him."

"I can't believe you did this. Why didn't you call the police?"

"They don't need to be involved so don't even think about running back inside. You and I are going to dispose of his body and that's the end of it."

"I can't believe this is happening."

"Well, believe it. Now shut up and get in the truck. We need to get back before your mother notices that we're missing."

This was worse than my worst nightmare. In my nightmare I was the one who died. I was the one gasping for air as a single bullet lodged its way into my heart. My killer was Julia though, not her dad. He was there with her, but she was the one who pulled the trigger. After she did it, the two of them sat on the edge of my bed hugging, rejoicing in my impending death. I repeated, "It was an accident," but they were either unable or unwilling to hear my final words. They just kept holding each other, relishing in their act of revenge.

"Damn it," my dad said as we turned left out of the alley. "Sit up and act natural."

Scanning the street left and right, I saw his point of concern. A police cruiser was approaching us and his emergency lights were flashing. My dad slowed the truck to a stop in the middle of the road.

"Hello, officer. I hope there isn't any trouble."

"Mr. Knutson, I thought that was you. Kind of late to be out for a drive," he said, leaning back to catch a glimpse of me in the passenger seat, "and with your son too?"

"We wanted to get a jump on our day. My neighbor recommended a new fishing spot a couple of hours that way," he said, pointing in no particular direction.

"Oh yeah? What's the name of it? I'm always looking for a new spot."

"I can't remember right off the top of my head. Lake Spear. Lake Speck. It's something similar to that. I can give you a ring when we get back in town."

"That would be mighty kind of you. Say, I have another question for you. Have you seen Michael Calhoun around your place this evening?"

"No sir."

"His car is parked not far from your house and I'm supposed to be keeping an eye on him tonight. You know," he fumbled, "with it being the anniversary of the death of his daughter and all."

"I haven't seen him." Turning toward me with a threatening look, he asked, "Peder, have you seen Mr. Calhoun this evening?"

I answered immediately. "No, I haven't seen him since this morning."

Motioning with his head in my direction, my dad went on to tell the officer that the situation with Michael this morning and the possibility of him returning this evening was another reason we were getting out of town at this hour. The officer must have bought my dad's story because he wished us good luck before driving away. Part of me hoped the officer saw through my dad's lies and followed us to wherever it was we were going. And what about Michael's SUV? Eventually someone was going to put two and two together.

I didn't say a word the rest of the trip. It had finally sunk in. I saw things for what they were. The man sitting beside me was nothing more than a monster, a killer, a murderer. I was ashamed to call him my dad. I didn't want to be related to someone so cold, someone so obsessed with protecting my mom and me that he was willing to break the law. Eh, forget the law, he was willing to take the life of a fellow human being and that was breaking some other kind of social and psychological law. That was the problem. My dad thought he was above the law, any and all of them.

43

"Kevin, a car just turned onto the road," I said excitedly, mere minutes after taking my second turn as the lookout. For the past hour or so, which I had to completely guess at because of our lack of cell phones and watches, the three of us took turns peering through a shattered window from inside the cabin. We were originally outside, but the mosquitoes were atrocious. Some of the blood suckers followed us in, but we were slowly killing them off.

"Let's get out of here then," Kevin said. "I'd rather be out in those trees than trapped in here. That hole is deep enough for a few more bodies."

I couldn't argue with that. Getting up to lead the way, I was saddened by the sight of Gabe. He hadn't moved a muscle since his last turn at the window. He had also been silent since we took shelter in the cabin and neither Kevin nor I urged him to come out of his shell. The thoughts and fears that he was probably having were something I couldn't relate to. I didn't think anyone could. His situation was unique to say the least.

Sitting down next to Gabe, I asked, "Are you coming with us?"

He shrugged his shoulders.

"Are you worried about your dad?"

Another non-verbal response.

"Gabe, no matter what happens tonight, it has nothing to do with you. You haven't done anything wrong. Your dad is very sick right now, so sick that he can't decipher right from wrong." I put my arm through his. "Come with us."

Without argument, he pushed himself up off the cabin floor. "He wants to make things right, to make things fair. He wants them to suffer as much as we have."

I silently rehearsed my reply as I led him out into the woods. My words weren't going to make him feel any better, but they needed to be said to clear my conscience if anything. "Killing an innocent child won't make it fair. It also won't change the situation, or the lives of anyone involved, for the better. No matter what your father is doing right now, he'll still be without his only daughter, and as harsh at it may sound, you'll still be that dead girl's brother."

Gabe looked at me in disbelief. My mother's honesty was shining through.

I continued. "Your sister's death was an accident. Peder doesn't deserve to die because of it."

"Try telling that to my dad," Gabe said before leaving my side to find a tree to take cover behind.

"I tried," I said too softly for him to hear. I did the best I could, but Gabe knew as well as I did that his dad was determined to even the score regardless of his own efforts to stop his compulsion to kill. Sometimes one's compulsion was just too strong.

The beams of light grew more intense as the vehicle approached. We hid on the far side this time, closer to the hole, or grave, depending on how you wanted to look at it. Being an optimist, I preferred to call it a hole. Because the cabin was blocking our view, we weren't able to catch a glimpse of the vehicle until it parked.

I knew something wasn't quite right when Kevin scurried from his tree to mine. To remain hidden from view, he held on to me from behind. "That's not Michael. That's not his SUV."

"What do you mean? Are you sure?" I hadn't expected anyone else to make an appearance. Did Michael hire a professional killer? Was someone helping him?

"The vehicle that pulled up is a truck. It's a pickup truck," Kevin said.

Panicked, I glanced in Gabe's direction to verify that he was still where he was supposed to be and to also ask for his assistance in identifying the owner of the truck. His expression was of pure horror. I turned back around to see what was so shocking and it was immediately clear to me. Mr. Knutson had just stepped out of the truck.

I felt a scream about to burst from my lungs. Kevin must have sensed it too because his hand quickly slammed over my mouth. His fingers tasted like dirt and sweat.

Wrenching his fingers away, I whispered, "This isn't good." I didn't know what else to say. I didn't know what to do. Never in a million years could I have predicted how this all was going to turn out. From our car crashing into the culvert to Mr. Knutson appearing in place of Michael, it was too much to handle. My grip on reality was escaping me and I wanted nothing more than to sit down right where I was and cry. I wanted to cry for Julia for dying before her time, for Gabe who didn't know what it was like to have a normal childhood, and for Peder who had to live with the eyes of the accusers for the rest of his life.

Adding fuel to the fire, I heard Mr. Knutson order, "Peder, get out of the truck."

Peder was here too? Was this an anniversary celebration and we didn't receive a formal invitation? Or maybe this was more of a private party. I was apprehensive to see the rest of the guest list.

Taking a moment to let it all soak in and to collect myself again, I said, "Kevin, I need to be with Gabe. Don't take your eyes off that truck."

"I wouldn't think of it," he replied.

I admired Kevin's strength and determination in tough situations like these. It made me feel guilty for giving him such a hard time and for not giving him the benefit of the doubt. He was one of the good guys and he deserved to be treated better, if not by me, then by someone else. That was something I needed to figure out when this was over. He deserved better.

As quiet as humanly possible when walking on a dirt path covered in dried, crunchy leaves, I tiptoed over to Gabe. He was leaning forward against the tree. His eyes were on the scenario playing out in front of him.

"Where's my dad?" Gabe whispered, not bothering to peel his eyes away.

"I don't know." I put my arm around his shoulders. That was my attempt at comforting someone who had been to hell and back and he wasn't even old enough to vote, or drive for that matter. I didn't know where his father was. I did know that Peder was alive. How the two of them intertwined was the bigger question.

Speaking of Peder, he was still sitting in the truck even after his father ordered him out. Mr. Knutson stood outside kicking pinecones while muttering phrases that were barely audible. Finally, fed up with his son's behavior, he stormed over to the passenger side door and yanked Peder out by his arm, making the poor kid land hard on his side.

"You're a monster! You're no better than he is!" Peder screamed, still lying on the ground.

Stepping back, Mr. Knutson said sternly, "I am better than he is. I put an end to this. I protected my family. You won't ever have to worry about waking up with a gun to your head ever again. You should be thanking me you ungrateful little shit."

"I'll never thank you! I hate you!"

"You don't mean that. Now get up," Mr. Knutson said, kicking his son. "You've got work to do."

Peder didn't budge.

"Get up!" Mr. Knutson shouted, bending down to get right in his son's face, "Or I'll make things a whole lot worse for you. You know I can."

This threat had Peder off the ground and following his father to the back of the truck. Mr. Knutson proceeded to open the tailgate and then reached in to pull out his prize, his prize for protecting his family.

"Here, Peder, you take his legs."

Without dispute, Peder reached into the truck. Together they pulled out Michael's dead body.

"Dad!" Gabe shouted.

Not thinking about the danger he was racing into, Gabe darted through the trees toward his father's body. My yelling for him to come back wasn't going to make a difference so I held my breath.

Gabe's screams halted the Knutson's. They stood a few feet from the truck holding Michael by his limbs. Peder was the first to let go. A half second later Michael's body was on the ground. Peder and his father rushed toward their truck. Afraid they were reaching for weapons, I took off after Gabe. My heart was beating so fast it hurt. I heard Kevin's footsteps coming up behind me, and then he passed me as we entered the clearing. We both stopped once our eyes met those of the new arrivals. As predicted, Mr. Knutson was wielding a shotgun while his son awkwardly held a knife. They took their places mere feet from Michael's bloodied body where Gabe lie across his father's chest mourning for his loss, the second major loss in his life. Gabe, with his hard exterior and threatening stares, wailed like a child, not like the man he sometimes pretended to be.

"I didn't know we were going to have company," Mr. Knutson said. "Now that he's here though we might as well put him in the dirt with his good-for-nothing father. He was next on my list anyway."

What a sick bastard. I knew something was off when I met him at his house, but this was beyond my comprehension.

"Hey, I recognize you," he said, pointing at me. "You came by my house the other day asking a bunch of questions. What do you have to do with this?" he asked.

Ignoring his question, I said, "You killed his father." My eyes weren't on the killer when I spoke. They were secured on Gabe, watching the emotion drain from his soul as he draped himself over the gash across his father's neck. No, Michael wasn't shot. His throat was slashed. Only a cold-blooded killer could take the life from a man using brute strength and a cold metal blade.

"He was coming after my son. He was stalking us, just like his waste of a sperm over there," Mr. Knutson said, pointing at Gabe. "I knew Michael came to our house late at night. He either sat outside in his car or crouched under my son's window. I know what goes on at my own home. I even got in my truck and followed him out here one night. It was a good thing too. He saved me a lot of work by digging his own grave. Of course, that's not why he did it. That grave was meant for Peder."

Peder's face exhibited no expression at the haunting words. He had surely heard it all before, probably on the drive out here. His father was proud of his actions, proud of how he had saved his son's life. I didn't deny him that Michael had dug the grave intending to put Peder's body in it, but it didn't have to end like this. Concerned family members and community agencies were eager to help both parties involved. Another life lost was not the answer.

"Michael deserved to die," Mr. Knutson continued, peering at me with hatred in his eyes. Kevin grabbed my hand and squeezed it as hard as he could. I hardly felt it though because every nerve in my body was consumed with fear.

Upon hearing Mr. Knutson's offensive last words, Gabe surprised us all by lunging with all his might at the big man holding the gun. His fury was enough to knock Mr. Knutson to the ground, releasing his grip on the rifle. Peder was quick to snatch it up while Gabe allowed his rage to temporarily overpower the man beneath him, clawing at his torso like a wild animal attacking its prey. It wasn't long before Mr. Knutson regained control and threw Gabe's gangly frame off him and into a nearby pile of rocks and leaves. While Gabe remained on the ground curled up and sobbing, Mr. Knutson got to his feet. His face and neck were badly scratched and bleeding.

"Give me that gun," Mr. Knutson barked, snatching it from his son's hands.

"Don't shoot him, Dad," Peder pleaded.

Kevin dropped my hand and bravely stepped out in between Mr. Knutson and Gabe. It was about time one of us entered the arena.

"Listen to your son. Gabe hasn't done anything wrong. He's just a kid."

"I was just a kid once too, but I didn't go around threatening families. He's no better than that piece of shit I'm about to bury," he replied. He used his shoulder to wipe away blood near his right eye.

Joining Kevin in the line of fire, I lied and said, "If you spare his life, we won't report this to the police. No one has to know about this but us."

"That's a bunch of bullshit and you know it. The first thing you'll do if you leave here is run to the cops. I'm not stupid."

Did he just say, "if you leave here?" Grappling with what to say next in the bargain for my life, a blur of flesh darted past my shoulder. Gabe was on the warpath again.

A shot was fired.

The warrior went down.

44

The sight of Peder huddled over Gabe's convulsing body remained engraved in my thoughts as Kevin and I darted through the trees to get as far away from the crime scene as possible. My legs ached, lungs burned, and heart bled for the possible loss of Gabe, but the desire to live to see another day drove my feet pounding into the dirt long after the sound of trailing footsteps diminished.

Slowing down a bit to catch my breath, I witnessed the sun rising over the horizon. It was a beautiful sight. There were times tonight when I questioned if I would ever see the sun again. We had been breathing in the darkness for hours, which was to our advantage when Mr. Knutson chased after us. He kept up much longer than I expected. Rage and the desire to get away with his crime must have given him the extra strength and longevity he needed. Our desire to live and tell about it was stronger. I had never run so fast and far in my life.

That was about to end.

"I'm done running, Kevin," I panted. "He probably turned around a long time ago."

"Yeah. I can't make it much longer either. We need to at least keep walking."

Setting our strides in sync, we continued our journey through a field of wildflowers, thorns and all, in the direction of the new day. The sound of birds singing and squirrels chattering filled the void left by our lack of conversation. We were too exhausted and too emotionally spent to start one, and honestly, where were we to begin?

About to enter another wooded area similar to the one we spent much of our night in, I broke the silence. "Do you think he's still alive? Gabe, I mean?"

"I don't know. I want to think he is, but then again Mr. Knutson wasn't going to go out of his way to help him. He shot to kill."

Kill. That word again.

"I feel terrible for leaving him there," I said as tears welled up in my eyes. Until now I had refrained from shedding a tear, but with our slowed pace I was able to reflect on everything that had happened over the past few hours. The flood walls were about to burst and there was nothing I could do to mend them, nor did I want to.

"We did the smart thing by getting out of there when we did," Kevin said, trying to console me. "Letting us live to retell the story wasn't an option."

"It doesn't matter," I said between sobs. "We left a child to die. We left him there. We chose to save ourselves instead." I dropped to the ground, too heavy with grief, too weak to continue. My heart was telling me that we made a mistake, that we should have stayed to fight the battle for Gabe's life. My mind urged me not to listen, saying that logically our night would have ended in a blood bath rendering the heart speechless. I understood both sides of the squabble; however I wasn't prepared to side with either one.

Kevin sat down beside me in the tall grass, lending me his shoulder to lean on if I wanted it. The gesture was generous and appreciated, but I needed to get through this on my own. I needed to make it right with me, not to say that I would ever feel good about our decision to leave. Until I knew in my heart that what *I* did was right, not Kevin, I would be an emotional mess. I cried until I was ready to stop.

* * * *

"...loud as you can," I heard a voice say, startling me out of my slumber. With my eyes wide open and my mind only half coherent, I was terrified to find myself huddled in a sea of prairie grass.

"Did you hear that?" I asked, jolting upright.

Kevin quickly yanked me back down. He looked as dazed and confused as I felt.

"Stay down," he said. "I'll check things out."

Chivalry. Okay, just this once.

I remained still, taking in the smell of the land and the view of the Minnesota sky while he slowly sat up to survey the area. My emotions were on the rise once again at the prospect of having to escape unscathed for the second time in less than twelve hours.

"I don't see anyone. Do you think we imagined it?" Kevin asked

"How could we both have imagined it?"

He shrugged his shoulders.

"Lie back down and let's listen again," I suggested.

While we waited, I gently patted my scorched skin. By way of the sun, it was almost noon, which meant we had been asleep for more than a couple of hours. It was hard to believe one could sleep after witnessing such horrific events, but the body took what it needed when it needed it. If only it could soak up water from the soil because according to my calculations, I was more than a little parched.

"Kody. Kody Burkoff. This is the police. If you can hear me, give me a signal," the omnipotent voice called out.

"Did you hear that?" I asked, jolting upright and away from Kevin for fear that he would knock me back down again.

"I heard it!" he shouted, standing all the way up. "They're looking for us. Say something, Kody. They want to hear your voice."

Skimming the area before rising to the occasion, I screamed "Help" as loud as my lungs allowed. Feeling left out, Kevin chimed in by screaming "Help" along with "We're here," "We're here by the field of blue flowers," and "I'm wearing a navy blue shirt." I had to chuckle at his last cry for help. It was crazy not to. With the long night behind us and rescuers hot on our trail, there was no reason not to be happy. Although, learning that Gabe was recuperating nicely in a hospital bed with his mother at his side would make it all the better.

45

"Did you locate the others?" I asked the officer first thing when he met us near a marshy area occupied by some native water fowl, or ducks, if you asked me. Where the officer originated from remained a mystery because from our vantage point there was no road in sight. To get to this spot, Kevin and I had to zigzag our way through fields and woods, following the voice registering through the megaphone. We, in turn, shouted for help until our voices went hoarse.

"What others? Do you mean the Knutson's?" the officer asked.

"Well, yes, but I'm more interested in Gabe Calhoun. Did you find him? Is he alive?"

"Yes, he's at the hospital. Last I heard he was going in for surgery."

Relief fell over me, so much so that tears filled my eyes again and I had to grab a hold of Kevin to keep from falling to the ground. I was so thankful to hear that Gabe had been rescued in time. I felt responsible for him being there. If Kevin and I hadn't picked him up, he would be hearing the news of his father's death from his mother. Instead, the image of his father's body being dropped carelessly to the ground as if his life had meant nothing will forever be ingrained in his memory. Some things a child should never see.

"Are you injured? Do you need medical attention?" the officer asked as he looked us over.

"No, I'm fine. Just thirsty," I replied.

Kevin concurred. "We're probably dehydrated, but that's the extent of our injuries, physically at least."

The officer handed us each a bottle of water and radioed back to the others on the rescue mission that we were recovered and uninjured.

Sure, on the outside we suffered from minor sunburns along with a few scratches on our arms and legs. Our psychological well-being was a whole different story. The images of watching Gabe get shot at close range were apt to haunt us for the rest of our lives. Or how about seeing Michael's body being dragged out from the back of a truck and then dropped to the ground like a bag of cement? That wasn't going away anytime soon. I had never before witnessed such vulgarity and lack of respect for a human being. Peder was right. His father was a monster.

"You think you can walk a little farther? Our vehicles are right over that hill."

"We can make it," Kevin said, grabbing on to my hand.

For once, I believed him.

* * * *

"He and Peder are in police custody," Investigator Dunn informed Kevin and me after we were treated for dehydration and released from the hospital.

"How did you find them?" I wanted to hear the whole story.

Dunn was seated across the table from us. This was the first time I had met the investigator in person and he looked nothing like what I had envisioned. His surfer blond hair and lanky frame seemed a better fit for a California beach, not a Minnesota police station.

"Our night patrol officer called me early this morning with suspicions that Mr. Knutson wasn't telling the truth when he told the officer he was leaving on a fishing trip with his son at around one thirty this morning. The officer also mentioned that Michael's SUV was in the vicinity of the Knutson's home, with no sign of Michael. The officer didn't put it all together right away so our response time was delayed more than I would have liked. Lucky for us though, an emergency volunteer that we called in to help saw Michael turn down County Road 32 a time or two. With nothing else to go on, we took that lead and ran with it.

"Another one of our volunteers used his spotlights and found a vehicle upended in the culvert. We checked the registration of the vehicle and saw that it was registered in Beaufort County. You, Ms. Burkoff, came immediately to mind. I had hoped you weren't stupid enough to try to tackle Michael's depression all on your own, but then again you definitely showed me your stubborn side during our phone conversations."

Kevin grimaced in pain as my elbow hit his ribs. "What was that for?" he asked, holding his side.

"For thinking about agreeing with him," I said playfully. To Dunn, I said, "I needed to do something. You weren't willing to commit twenty-four-hour surveillance so I took it on myself to fill the need. I wanted to prevent Michael from doing something he would later regret and protect Peder at the same time. I never figured on Michael becoming the victim."

"None of us did," Dunn agreed. "About your car, that was quite a tumble you took. Why that bridge doesn't have a guard rail on either side of it is beyond me. You're awfully lucky you didn't get injured in the fall."

"It scared us more than anything," Kevin said.

Dunn nodded and then continued. "Seeing your vehicle confirmed our suspicions that something was going on at the old Winston cabin. I instructed our officers to have their guns ready.

Records showed that Mr. Knutson had a registered handgun and I didn't want any of our men to go out there unprepared.

"Surprisingly, Mr. Knutson was holding a rifle when we pulled up. His son wasn't far from him, kneeling on the ground next to Gabe Calhoun. It took some convincing to get Mr. Knutson to drop his weapon. He still thought he could get away with his crime even though he was surrounded. His son eventually intervened and talked some sense into him. Peder said something about the family being safe now that Michael was gone. It was a good thing too because we were ready to shoot since it was evident that Gabe was in need of medical attention. In fact, I thought we had arrived too late."

"I'm shocked he didn't put up more of a fight," I chimed in. "He was going to kill us. I don't know how far he chased after us through those woods."

"He's not saying much. I was in the interrogation room with him before I came in here to talk to you and he wouldn't answer any of my questions."

"The evidence says it all," I said, feeling like the criminal investigator I had watched a million times on television.

"That it does," Dunn agreed. "Well, I know you two are probably eager to get home and get some shut-eye. You endured a long night." He stood up and outstretched his hand. "I want to thank you for doing what you did. If you hadn't followed Mr. Knutson down that dirt road, we might never have found Michael's body."

I shook his hand first. "Dragging Gabe into the mess didn't turn out the best, but I'm glad he's going to be okay."

Kevin stood up to shake Dunn's hand and added, "I think we'll stop by the hospital for a visit before we leave. We should give our condolences to him and his mom."

46

"Mrs. Calhoun called me last night. Gabe is doing well and will be going home tomorrow."

"That's good to hear," Kevin said, his mouth full of food.

It was Friday night and it was Kevin's turn to choose the restaurant. He, of course, chose pizza. Remember what I said about him being so predictable? He was still allowing us to have a label-free relationship though so eating pizza was the least I could do.

"She also mentioned that Mr. Knutson's trial will be some time next winter. Won't that be fun for us?"

"I like when you say us," he said with a cheesy grin.

I rolled my eyes. It was a natural reaction at this point. Ever since we returned from the woods that life-altering night, Kevin has been overly-attentive to my every want and need. He jumped when I asked for a drink of water. He sprinted over when I invited him to my place to watch a movie. He went above and beyond the call of duty for a boyfriend who wasn't my boyfriend. Some days I liked it. Some days I didn't. And some days I thought about Paul.

Paul has called a few times since he spent the night on my couch. I never did mention that evening to Kevin. Can you imagine the long, in-depth conversation he would require of me to reassure him that there was nothing going on between Paul and me? Not my idea of a good time.

On the phone, Paul and I chatted like old buddies. He told me stories about friends he was catching up with at home and about how his dad was micro-managing his every move at the hardware store. Not once had he come close to asking me out. He hadn't mentioned dating anyone else either for that matter. The single ladies were probably waiting with baited breath for him to join the dating scene. Hopefully Becky Flick wouldn't sink her teeth into him and take him as part of her harem.

Part of me wanted Paul to ask me out, but then part of me wanted him to keep his distance to give Kevin and me a chance. Realistically speaking, however many chances Kevin and I might have, it would never compare to my first flirtation with love. Arguably, whether or not Paul was my first true love, he would always be an important part of my past.

"Kody? Are you still with me? What was that story you wanted to tell me about Mrs. Lopez?" Kevin asked.

"Oh, you are going to love this," I said, clearing my thoughts. "Remember, you can't tell another soul." I was going straight to hell for sharing so many client stories lately.

"I promise."

"This is a crazy story. Sad too. I can't even believe this sort of thing happens, and at his age."

"Just tell me already."

"Okay. Mrs. Lopez was seeing this man whom she thought was perfect in every way. I mean, she crooned over him. He was sweet, charming, endearing, and spontaneous. He was the most perfect man she had met since her late husband."

"Perfect isn't always perfect," Kevin grumbled.

Um, okay.

"Last Tuesday during bingo night at the senior citizen center, Mr. Perfect did something to completely change her mind about him. I can't even believe I'm saying this."

"Go on."

"Okay. Donning nothing but a black trench coat, this young man of eighty-three walked into the building, flung open his coat, and streaked past the bingo players, both women and men. He was buck naked."

"You're kidding."

"No. I couldn't make that up."

"Why would he do that?"

"You've got me. Mrs. Lopez said he was a bit mysterious. That was one of the qualities she liked about him."

Pushing his last slice of pizza away, he said, "That's disturbing to say the least."

"You don't think you'll try something like that?" I joked.

"If I do, divorce me."

Here we go again.

"Are you about ready to get out of here? We can talk about divorce another night."

Dodging another awkward conversation with my overzealous admirer, I flagged down the waitress to get our check. I wasn't ready to talk engagement, marriage, or divorce with Kevin. He, on the other hand, already had us walking down the aisle. I don't know what went through his mind while we were in the woods with the Calhoun's and Knutson's, but I was taking the full brunt of it. I guess that's what happens when you're in a semi-relationship with a guy without a family. Kevin needed someone and I was all he had.

We walked out of the restaurant and I refused Kevin's offer to snuggle on his couch. I needed some space this evening. I was feeling smothered. Kevin knew it too because he didn't ask a second time. He had learned when to back off, much like Mary with her husband. Mary no longer badgered him about where he was going or where he had been. She overlooked his absence while trying to maintain her focus on herself. Mary needed to fix Mary before attempting to fix her marriage, if it was even worth the effort. I wouldn't be surprised if her husband left her one of these days. He had seemed to move on without her. It's too bad too because I got the impression she had visions of them reconciling their love. She never said that, but I could tell that was what she was thinking.

Alone with my thoughts and too tired to sleep, I created a cozy spot on the couch and flipped through the channels. How much did I pay for cable and not a single show grabbed my attention?

My phone rang. Apparently I wasn't the only one unable to sleep.

"Did I wake you?"

"Nah. I can't sleep. You either?"

"No. I ran into Clyde Dextrom this afternoon," Paul started, "and I thought of you when he told me about his mobile home disaster. He's always been such a hillbilly."

I laughed along with Paul, remembering the likes of Clyde. I also laughed at Paul's enthusiasm when he told Clyde's story. I loved that about him. I loved a lot of things about him. Was it possible that when combined, Paul and Kevin had all the qualities I was looking for in a man? Sure, it was possible. Anything was possible.

47

To: kodyburkoff@inyourwords.com
From: sad_dad1@gmail.com
Subject: It's not over

It didn't end right. Peder's still a free man. I'm still a prisoner of my grief. My mom thinks everything is fine and that we'll come out of this better than when Julia was killed. I don't know why she says that. It makes me angry. I don't think I'll ever stop being angry. I don't think I'll ever stop wanting to kill him.

Care to help me like you helped my dad?

ABOUT THE AUTHOR

Jennifer L. Davidson is the author of *Missing Maggie*. This is her second novel. She lives in southeastern Minnesota with her husband and three children.

15399701R00134

Made in the USA
Charleston, SC
01 November 2012